Ronald Firbank

TWO NOVELS

The Flower
Beneath The Foot

Prancing Nigger

WITH A CHRONOLOGY
by Miriam K. Benkovitz

A NEW DIRECTIONS PAPERBOOK

CONTENTS

Published under arrangement with
the Ronald Firbank Estate

First published as ND Paperbook 128 in 1962
First Printing

Manufactured in the United States of America
Printed by The Murray Printing Company
New Directions Books are published by James Laughlin at
Norfolk, Connecticut. New York Office: 333 Sixth Avenue (14).

The Flower

Beneath The Foot

Being a Record of the Early Life of
St. Laura de Nazianzi and the
Times in Which She Lived

"Some girls are born organically good : I wasn't."
ST LAURA DE NAZIANZI.

"It was about my eighteenth year that I conquered my *Ego*."
IBID.

I

NEITHER her Gaudiness the Mistress
of the Robes, or her Dreaminess the
Queen were feeling quite themselves.
In the Palace all was speculation. Would
they be able to attend the *Fêtes* in honour
of King Jotifa, and Queen Thleeanouhee
of the Land of Dates?—Court opinion
seemed largely divided. Countess Medusa
Rappa, a woman easily disturbable, was
prepared to wager what the Countess of
Tolga "liked" (she knew), that another
week would find the Court shivering beneath the vaulted domes of the Summer-
Palace.

"I fear I've no time (or desire) now,
Medusa," the Countess answered, moving
towards the Royal apartments, "for
making bets," though turning before the
ante-room door she nodded: "Done!"

She found her sovereign supine on a
couch piled with long Tunisian cushions,

9

while a maid of honour sat reading to her aloud :

" *Live with an aim, and let that aim be high !* " the girl was saying as the Countess approached.

" Is that you, Violet ? " her Dreaminess enquired without looking round.

" How is your condition, Madam ? " the Countess anxiously murmured.

" Tell me, do, of a place that soothes and lulls one—— ? "

The Countess of Tolga considered.

" Paris," she hazarded.

" Ah ! Impossible."

" The Summer-Palace, then," the Countess ejaculated, examining her long slender fingers that were like the tendrils of a plant.

" Dr Cuncliffe Babcock flatly forbids it," the Royal woman declared, starting slightly at the sound of a gun : " That must be *the Dates !* " she said. And in effect, a vague reverberation, as of individuals cheering, resounded fitfully from afar. " Give me my diamond anemones," the Queen commanded, and motioning to her Maid : " Pray conclude, mademoiselle, those lofty lines."

With a slight sigh, the lectress took up the posture of a Dying Intellectual.

"*Live with an aim, and let that aim be high!*" she reiterated in tones tinged perceptibly with emotion.

" But not *too* high, remember, Mademoiselle de Nazianzi . . ."

There was a short pause. And then—

" Ah Madam ! What a dearest he is ! "

" I think you forget yourself," the Queen murmured with a quelling glance. " You had better withdraw."

" He has such strength ! One could niche an idol in his dear, dinted chin."

" Enough ! "

And a moment later, the enflamed girl left the room warbling softly : *Depuis le Jour.*

" Holy Virgin," the Countess said, addressing herself to the ceiling. " Should his Weariness, the Prince, yield himself to this caprice . . ."

The Queen shifted a diamond bangle from one of her arms to the other.

"She reads at such a pace," she complained, "and when I asked her *where* she had learnt to read so quickly, she replied 'On the screens at Cinemas.'"

"I do not consider her at all distinguished," the Countess commented turning her eyes away towards the room.

It was a carved-ceiled, and rather lofty room, connected by tall glass doors with other rooms beyond. Peering into one of these the Countess could see reflected the "throne," and a little piece of broken Chippendale brought from England, that served as a stand for a telephone, wrought in ormolu and rock-crystal, which the sun's rays at present were causing to emit a thousand playful sparks. Tapestry panels depicting the Loves of *Mejnoun and Leileh* half concealed the silver *boisèries* of the walls, while far down the room, across old rugs from Chirvan that were a marvellous wonder, showed fortuitous jardinières, filled with every flowering-kind of plant. Between the windows were canopied recesses, denuded of their statues by the Queen's desire, "in order that they might appear suggestive," while through the windows themselves, the Countess could catch across the fore-court of the castle, a panorama of the town below, with the State Theatre and the Garrisons, and the Houses of Parliament, and the Hospital, and the low white dome, crowned by turquoise-tinted tiles of the Cathedral, which was known to all churchgoers as *the Blue Jesus*.

"It would be a fatal connexion," the Queen continued, "and it must never, never be!"

By way of response the Countess exchanged with her sovereign a glance that was known in Court circles as her *tortured-animal* look: "Their Oriental majesties," she observed, "to judge from the din, appear to have already endeared themselves with the mob!"

The Queen stirred slightly amid her cushions.

"For the aggrandisement of the country's trade, an alliance with Dateland is by no means to be depreciated," she replied, closing her eyes as though in some way or other this bullion to the State would allow

13

her to gratify her own wildest whims, the
dearest, perhaps, of which was to form a
party to excavate (for objects of art)
among the ruins of Chedorlahomor, a
faubourg of Sodom.

"Am I right, Madam, in assuming it's
Bananas? . . ." the Countess queried.

But at that moment the door opened,
and his Weariness the Prince entered the
room in all his tinted Orders.

Handsome to tears, his face, even as a
child had lacked innocence. His was of
that *magnolia* order of colouring, set off
by pleasantly untamed eyes, and teeth like
flawless pearls.

"You've seen them? What are they
like. . . . Tell Mother, darling?" the
Queen exclaimed.

"They're merely dreadful," his Weariness,
who had been to the railway-station to
welcome the Royal travellers, murmured
in a voice extinct with boredom.

"They're in European dress, dear?"
his mother questioned.

"The King had on a frock coat and a
cap. . . ."

" And she ? "

" A tartan-skirt, and checked wool-stockings."

" She has great individuality, so I hear, marm," the Countess ventured.

" Individuality be —— ! No one can doubt she's a terrible woman."

The Queen gently groaned.

" I see life to-day," she declared, " in the colour of mould."

The Prince protruded a shade the purple violet of his tongue.

" Well, it's depressing," he said, " for us all, with the Castle full of blacks."

" That is the least of my worries," the Queen observed. " Oh, Yousef, Yousef," she added, " do you wish to break my heart ? "

The young man protruded some few degrees further his tongue.

" I gather you're alluding to Laura ! " he remarked.

" But what can you *see* in her ? " his mother mourned.

" She suits my feelings," the Prince simply said.

" Peuh ! "

" She meets my needs."

" She's so housemaid. . . . I hardly know . . . ! " the Queen raised beautiful hands bewildered.

" Très gutter, ma'am," the Countess murmured dropping her voice to a half-whisper.

" She saves us from *cliché*," the Prince indignantly said.

" She saves us from nothing," his mother returned. " Oh, Yousef, Yousef. And what *cerné* eyes, my son. I suppose you were gambling all night at the Château des Fleurs ? "

" Just hark to the crowds ! " the Prince evasively said. And never too weary to receive an ovation, he skipped across the room towards the nearest window, where he began blowing kisses to the throng.

" Give them the Smile Extending, darling," his mother beseeched.

" Won't you rise and place your arm about him, Madam," the Countess suggested.

" I'm not feeling at all up to the mark," her Dreaminess demurred, passing her fingers over her hair.

"There is sunshine, ma'am . . . and you have your *anemones* on . . ." the Countess cajoled, "and to please the people, you ought indeed to squeeze him." And she was begging and persuading the Queen to rise, as the King entered the room preceded by a shapely page (of sixteen) with cheeks fresher than milk.

"Go to the window, Willie," the Queen exhorted her Consort fixing an eye on the last trouser button that adorned his long, straggling legs.

The King, who had the air of a tired pastry-cook, sat down.

"We feel," he said, "to-day, we've had our fill of stares!"

"One little bow, Willie," the Queen entreated, "that wouldn't kill you."

"We'd give perfect worlds," the King went on, "to go, by Ourselves, to bed."

"Get rid of the noise for me. *Quiet them*. Or I'll be too ill," the Queen declared, "to leave my room to-night!"

"Should I summon Whisky, Marm?" the Countess asked, but before there was time to reply the Court physician, Dr Cuncliffe Babcock was announced.

"I feel I've had a relapse, Doctor," her Dreaminess declared.

Dr Babcock beamed: he had one blind eye—though this did not prevent him at all from seeing all that was going on with the other.

"Leave it to me, Madam," he assured, "and I shall pick you up in *no* time!"

"Not Johnnie, doctor?" the Queen murmured with a grimace. For a glass of *Johnnie Walker* at bed-time was the great doctor's favourite receipt.

"No; something a little stronger, I think."

"We need expert attention, too," the King intervened.

"You certainly are somewhat pale, sir."

"Whenever I go out," the King complained, "I get an impression of raised hats."

It was seldom King William of Pisuerga spoke in the singular tense, and Doctor Babcock looked perturbed.

" Raised hats, sir ? " he murmured in impressive tones.

" Nude heads, doctor."

The Queen commenced to fidget. She disliked that the King should appear more interesting than herself.

" These earrings tire me," she said, " take them out."

But the Prince, who seemed to be thoroughly enjoying the success of his appearance with the crowd, had already begun tossing the contents of the flower vases into the street.

"Willie . . . prevent him ! Yousef . . . I forbid you !" her Dreaminess faintly shrieked. And to stay her son's despoiling hand she skimmed towards him, when the populace catching sight of her, redoubled their cheers.

Meanwhile Mademoiselle de Nazianzi had regained again her composure. A niece of her Gaudiness the Mistress of the Robes (the Duchess of Cavaljos), her recent début at Court, had been made under the brightest conceivable of conditions.

Laura Lita Carmen Etoile de Nazianzi

was more piquant perhaps than pretty. A dozen tiny moles were scattered about her face, while on either side of her delicate nose, a large grey eye surveyed the world with a pensive critical glance.

" Scenes like that make one sob with laughter," she reflected, turning into the corridor where two of the Maids of Honour, like strutting idols, were passing up and down.

" Is she really very ill? Is she *really* dying? " they breathlessly enquired.

Mademoiselle de Nazianzi disengaged herself from their solicitously entwining arms.

" She is not ! " she answered, in a voice full of eloquent inflections.

But beguiled by the sound of marching feet, one of the girls had darted forward towards a window.

" Oh Blanche, Blanche, Blanchie love ! " she exclaimed, " I could dance to the click of your brother's spurs. "

" You'd not be the first to dear darling ! " Mademoiselle de Lambèse replied, adjusting her short shock of hair before a glass.

THE FLOWER BENEATH THE FOOT

Mademoiselle de Lambèse believed herself to be a very valuable piece of goods, and seemed to think she had only to smile to stir up an Ocean of passion.

" Poor Ann-Jules," she said : " I fear he's in the clutches of that awful woman."

" Kalpurnia ? "

" Every night he's at the Opera."

" I hear she wears the costume of a shoe-black in the new ballet," Mademoiselle de Nazianzi said, " and is too strangely extraordinary ! "

" Have you decided, Rara,[1] yet, what you'll wear for the ball ? "

" A black gown and three blue flowers on my tummy."

" After a Shrimp-tea with the Arch-duchess, I feel I *want* no dinner," Mademoiselle Olga Blumenghast, a girl with slightly hunched shoulders said, returning from the window.

" Oh ? Had she a party ? "

" A curé or two, and the Countess Yvorra."

[1] The name by which the future saint was sometimes called among her friends.

" Her black bordered envelopes make one shiver ! "

" I thought I should have died it was so dull," Mademoiselle Olga Blumenghast averred, standing aside to allow his Lankiness, Prince Olaf (a little boy wracked by all the troubles of Spring), and Mrs Montgomery, the Royal Governess to pass. They had been out evidently among the crowd, and both were laughing heartily at the asides they had overheard.

" 'Ow can you be so frivolous, your royal 'ighness ? " Mrs Montgomery was expostulating : " for shame, wicked boy ! For shame ! " And her cheery British laugh echoed gaily down the corridors.

" Well *I* took tea at the Ritz," Mademoiselle de Lambèse related.

" Anybody ? "

" Quite a few ! "

" There's a rumour that Prince Yousef is entertaining there to-night."

Mademoiselle Blumenghast tittered.

" Did you hear what he called the lanterns for the *Fête* ? " she asked.

" No."

THE FLOWER BENEATH THE FOOT

" A lot of ' bloody bladders ' ! "

" What, what a dearest," Mademoiselle de Nazianzi sighed beneath her breath. And all along the almost countless corridors as far as her bedroom door, she repeated again and again : " What, *what* a dearest ! "

II

BENEATH a wide golden ceiling people were dancing. A capricious concert waltz, drowsy, intricate, caressing, reached fitfully the supper-room, where a few privileged guests were already assembled to meet King Jotifa and Queen Thleeanouhee of the Land of Dates.

It was one of the regulations of the Court, that those commanded to the King's board, should assemble some few minutes earlier than the Sovereigns themselves, and the guests at present were mostly leaning stiffly upon their chair-backs, staring vacuously at the olives and salted almonds upon the table-cloth before them. Several of the ladies indeed had taken the liberty to seat themselves, and were beguiling the time by studying the menu or disarranging the smilax, while one dame went as far as to take, and even to nibble, a salted almond. A conversation of a non-private kind (carried on between the thin, authoritative legs of a Court Chamberlain) by Countess Medusa Rappa and the English Ambassadress, was being listened to by some with mingled signs of interest.

" Ah ! How clever Shakespere ! " the Countess was saying : " How gorgeous ! How glowing ! I once knew a speech from ' Julia Sees Her ! . . .' perhaps his greatest *œuvre* of all. Yes ! ' Julia *Sees* Her ' is what I like best of that great, great master."

The English Ambassadress plied her fan.

" Friends, Comrades, Countrymen," she murmured, " I used to know it myself ! "

But the lady nibbling almonds was exciting a certain amount of comment. This was the Duchess of Varna, voted by many to be one of the handsomest women of the Court. Living in economical obscurity nearly half the year round, her appearances at the palace were becoming more and more infrequent.

" I knew the Varnas were very hard up, but I did not know they were *starving*," the Countess Yvorra, a woman with a

would-be indulgent face, that was something less hard than rock, remarked to her
neighbour the Count of Tolga, and dropping
her glance from the Count's weak chin she
threw a fleeting smile towards his wife,
who was looking " Eastern " swathed in
the skin of a blue panther.

" Yes, their affairs it seems are almost
desperate," the Count returned, directing
his gaze towards the Duchess.

Well-favoured beyond measure she
certainly was, with her immense placid
eyes, and bundles of loose, blonde hair.
She had a gown the green of Nile water,
that enhanced to perfection the swan-like
fairness of her throat and arms.

" I'm thinking of building myself a Villa
in the Land of Dates ! " she was confiding
to the British Ambassador, who was standing beside her on her right : " Ah, yes !
I shall end my days in a country strewn
with flowers."

" You would find it I should say too hot,
Duchess."

" My soul has need of the sun, Sir Somebody ! " the Duchess replied, opening with

26

equanimity a great black ostrich fan, and smiling up at him through the sticks.

Sir Somebody Something was a person whose nationality was written all over him. Nevertheless, he had despite a bluff, and somewhat rugged manner, a certain degree of feminine sensitiveness, and any reference to the *soul* at all (outside the Embassy Chapel), invariably made him fidget.

" In moderation, Duchess," he murmured, fixing his eyes upon the golden head of a champagne bottle.

" They say it is a land of love ! " the Duchess related, raising indolently an almond to her sinuously-chiselled lips.

" And even, so it's said, too," his Excellency returned : " of licence ! " when just at this turn of things the Royal cortège entered the supper-room, to the exhilarating strains of King Goahead's War-March.

Those who had witnessed the arrival of King Jotifa and his Queen earlier in the afternoon, were amazed at the alteration of their aspect now. Both had discarded their European attire for the loosely-flowing vestments of their native land, and for a brief while there was some slight confusion among those present as to which was the gentleman, or which the lady of the two. The king's beard long and blonde, should have determined the matter outright, but on the other hand the Queen's necklet of reeds and plumes was so very misleading. . . . Nobody in Pisuerga, had seen anything to compare to it before. " Marvellous, though terrifying," the Court passed verdict.

Attended by their various suites, the royal party gained their places amid the usual manifestation of loyal respect.

But one of the Royal ladies as it soon became evident was not yet come.

" Where's Lizzie, Lois ? " King William asked, riveting the Archduchess' empty chair.

" We'd better begin without her Willie," the Queen exclaimed, " you know she never minds."

And hardly had the company seated themselves when, dogged by a lady-in-waiting and a maid-of-honour, the Archduchess Elizabeth of Pisuerga rustled in.

THE FLOWER BENEATH THE FOOT

Very old and very bent, and (even) very beautiful, she was looking as the Grammar-books say, ' meet ' to be robbed, beneath a formidable tiara, and a dozen long strands of pearls.

" Forgive me Willie," she murmured, with a little high shrill tinkling laugh : " but it was so fine, that after tea I, and a Lady, went paddling in the Basin of the Nymphs."

" How was the water ? " the King enquired.

The Archduchess repressed a sneeze : " Fresh," she replied, " but not too . . ."

" After sunset, beware dear Aunt, of chills."

" But for a frog, I believe nothing would have got me out ! " the august lady confessed as she fluttered bird-like to her chair.

Forbidden in youth by parents and tutors alike the joys of paddling under pain of chastisement, the Archduchess Elizabeth appeared to find a zest in doing so now. Attended by a chosen lady-in-waiting (as a rule the dowager Marchioness of Lallah Miranda) she liked to slip off to

one of the numerous basins or natural
grottos in the castle gardens, where she
would pass whole hours in wading blissfully
about. Whilst paddling, it was her wont
to run over those refrains from the vaude-
villes and operas (with their many shakes
and rippling *cadenzi*), in favour in her day,
interspersed at intervals by such cries as :
" Pull up your skirt, Marquise, it's dragging
a little my friend below the knees . . ." or,
" A shark, a shark ! " which was her way
of designating anything that had fins, from
a carp to a minnow.

" I fear our Archduchess has contracted
a slight catarrh," the Mistress of the Robes,
a woman like a sleepy cow, observed,
addressing herself to the Duke of Varna
upon her left.

" Unless she is more careful, she'll go
paddling once too often," the Duke replied,
contemplating with interest, above the
moonlight-coloured daffodils upon the table
board, one of the button-nosed belles of
Queen Thleeanouhee's suite. The young
creature, referred to cryptically among the
subordinates of the Castle, as ' Tropical

Molly,' was finding fault already it seemed with the food.

"Take it away," she was protesting in animated tones : "I'd as soon touch a foot-squashed mango!"

"No *mayonnaise*, miss?" a court-official asked, dropping his face prevailingly to within an inch of her own.

"Take it right away. . . . And if you should *dare* sir! to come any closer . . . !"

The Mistress of the Robes fingered nervously the various Orders of Merit on her sumptuous bosom.

"I trust there will be no contretemps," she murmured, glancing uneasily towards the Queen of the Land of Dates, who seemed to be lost in admiration of the Royal dinner-service of scarlet plates, that looked like pools of blood upon the cloth.

"What pleases me in your land," she was expansively telling her host, "is less your food, than the china you serve it on ; for with us you know there's none. And now," she added, marvellously wafting a fork, "I'm for ever spoilt for shells."

King William was incredulous.

" With you no china ? " he gasped.

" None, Sir, none ! "

" I could not be more astonished," the king declared, " if you told me there were fleas at the Ritz," a part of which assertion Lady Something, who was blandly listening, imperfectly chanced to hear.

" Who would credit it ! " she breathed, turning to an attaché, a young man all white and pensieroso, at her elbow.

" Credit what ? "

" Did you not hear what the dear king said ! "

" No."

" It's almost *too* appalling . . ." Lady Something replied, passing a small, nerveless hand across her brow.

" Won't you tell me though," the young man murmured gently, with his nose in his plate.

Lady Something raised a glass of frozen lemonade to her lips.

" Fleas," she murmured, " have been found at the Ritz."

" . . . . ! . . . . ? . . . . ! . . . . . !!! "

"Oh and *poor* Lady Bertha! And poor good old Mrs Hunter!" And Lady Something looked away in the direction of Sir Somebody, as though anxious to catch his eye.

But the British Ambassador and the Duchess of Varna were weighing the chances of a Grant being allowed by Parliament for the excavation of Chedorlahomor.

"Dear little Chedor," the Duchess kept on saying, "I'm sure one would find the most enthralling things there. Aren't *you*, Sir Somebody?"

And they were still absorbed in their colloquy when the King gave the signal to rise.

Although King William had bidden several distinguished Divas from the Opera House to give an account of themselves for the entertainment of his guests, both King Jotifa and Queen Thleeanouhee with disarming candour declared that, to their ears, the music of the West was hardly to be borne.

"Well I'm not very fond of it either," her Dreaminess admitted, surrendering her

33

skirts to a couple of rosy boys, and leading the way with airy grace towards an adjacent salon, "although," she wistfully added across her shoulder, to a high dignitary of the Church, " I'm trying it's true, to coax the dear Archbishop to give the first act of *La Tosca* in the Blue Jesus. . . . Such a perfect setting, and with Desiré Erlinger and Maggie Mellon . . . ! "

And as the Court now pressed after her the rules of etiquette became considerably relaxed. Mingling freely with his guests, King William had a hand-squeeze and a fleeting word for each.

" In England," he paused to enquire of Lady Something, who was warning a dowager, with impressive earnestness, against the Ritz, "have you ever seen two cooks in a kitchen-garden ? "

" No, never, sir ! " Lady Something simpered.

" Neither," the King replied moving on, " have *we*."

The Ambassadress beamed.

" My dear," she told Sir Somebody, a moment afterwards, " my dear, the King was simply charming. Really I may say he was more than gracious ! He asked me if I had ever seen two cooks in a kitchen-garden, and I said no, never ! And he said that neither, either, had he ! And oh isn't it so strange how few of us ever have ? "

But in the salon, one of Queen Thlee-anouhee's ladies had been desired by her Dreaminess to sing.

" It seems so long," she declared, "since I heard an Eastern voice, and it would be such a relief."

" By all means," Queen Thleeanouhee said, " and let a *darbouka* or two be brought ! For what charms the heart more, what touches it more," she asked, considering meditatively her babouched feet, " than a *darbouka* ? "

It was told that, in the past, her life had been a gallant one, although her adventures, it was believed, had been mostly with men. Those however, who had observed her conduct closely, had not failed to remark how often her eyes had been attracted in the course of the evening towards the dimpled cheeks of the British Ambassadress.

Perceiving her ample form not far away, Queen Thleeanouhee signalled to her amiably to approach.

Née Rosa Bark (and a daughter of the Poet) Lady Something was perhaps not sufficiently tactful to meet all the difficulties of the rôle in which it had pleased life to call her. But still, she tried, and did do her best, which often went far to retrieve her lack of *savoir faire.* " Life is like that, dear," she would sometimes say to Sir Somebody, but she would never say what it was that life was like, ' *That,*' it seemed. . . .

" I was just looking for my daughter," she declared.

" And is she as sympathetic," Queen Thleeanouhee softly asked, " as her mamma ? "

" She's shy—of the Violet persuasion, but that's not a bad thing in a young girl."

" Where *I* reign, shyness is a quality which is entirely unknown. . . . ! "

" It must be astonishing, ma'am," Lady

36

Something replied, caressing a parure of
false jewels, intended, indeed, to deceive
no one, "to be a Queen of a sun-steeped
country like yours."

Queen Thleeanouhee fetched a sigh.

" Dateland—my dear, it's a scorch ! "
she averred.

" I conclude, ma'am, it's what *we* should
call ' conservatory ' scenery ? " Lady Something murmured.

" It is the land of the jessamine-flower,
the little amorous jessamine-flower," the
Queen gently cooed with a sidelong smiling
glance, "that twines itself sometimes to
the right-hand, at others to the left, just
according to its caprices ! "

" It sounds I fear to be unhealthy,
ma'am."

" And it is the land also, of romance, my
dear, where *shyness* is a quality which is
entirely unknown," the Queen broke off,
as one of her ladies, bearing a *darbouka*,
advanced with an air of purposefulness
towards her.

The hum of voices which filled the room
might well have tended to dismay a vocalist
of modest powers, but the young matron

known to the Court as 'Tropical Molly,' and whom her mistress addressed as Timzra, soon shewed herself to be equal to the occasion.

> " Under the blue gum-tree
> I am sitting waiting,
> Under the blue gum-tree
> I am waiting all alone ! "

Her voice reached the ears of the fresh-faced ensigns and the beardless subalterns in the Guard Room far beyond, and startled the pages in the distant dormitories, as they lay smoking on their beds.

And then, the theme changing, and with an ever-increasing passion, fervour and force :

> " I heard a Watch-dog in the night . . .
> Wailing, wailing . . .
> Why is the watch-dog wailing ?
> He is wailing for the Moon ! "

" That is one of the very saddest songs," the King remarked, " that I have ever heard. ' Why is the watchdog wailing ? He is wailing for the Moon ! ' " And the ambitions and mortifications of kingship, for a moment weighed visibly upon him.

"Something merrier, Timzra!" Queen Thleeanouhee said.

And throwing back her long love-lilac sleeves, Timzra sang:

"A negress with a margaret once, lolled
    frousting in the sun
Thinking of all the little things that she
    had left undone . . .
With a hey, hey, hey, hey, hi, hey ho!"

"She has the air of a cannibal!" the Archduchess murmured behind her fan to his Weariness, who had scarcely opened his lips except to yawn throughout the whole of the evening.

"She has the air of a ——" he replied, laconically, turning away.

Since the conversation with his mother earlier in the day, his thoughts had revolved incessantly around Laura. What had they been saying to the poor wee witch, and whereabouts was she to be found?

Leaving the salon, in the wake of a pair of venerable politicians, who were helping each other along with little touches and pats, he made his way towards the ball-room, where a new dance known as the Pisgah Pas was causing some excitement, and gaining a post of vantage, it was not long before he caught a glimpse of the agile, boyish figure of his betrothed. She passed him, without apparently noticing he was there, in a whirlwind of black tulle, her little hand pressed to the breast of a man like a sulky eagle ; and he could not help rejoicing inwardly, that, *once* his wife, it would no longer be possible for her to enjoy herself exactly with whom she pleased. As she swept by again he succeeded in capturing her attention, and nodding mean-ingly towards a deserted picture-gallery, wandered away towards it. It was but seldom he set foot there, and he amused himself by examining some of the pictures to be seen upon the walls. An old shrew with a rose . . . a drawing of a man alone in the last extremes . . . a pink-robed Christ . . . a seascape, painted probably in winter, with cold, hard colouring . . .

" Yousef ? "

" Rara ! "

" Let us go outside, dear."

A night so absolutely soft and calm, was delicious after the glare and noise within.

" With whom," he asked, " sweetheart, were you last dancing ? "

" Only the brother of one of the Queen's Maids, dear," Mademoiselle de Nazianzi replied. " After dinner, though," she tittered, " when he gets Arabian-Nighty, it's apt to annoy one a scrap ! "

" *Arabian-Nighty ?* "

" Oh, never mind ! "

" But (pardon me dear) I do."

" Don't be tiresome, Yousef ! The night is too fine," she murmured glancing absently away towards the hardly moving trees, from whose branches a thousand drooping necklets of silver lamps palely burned.

Were *those* the " bladders " then ?

Strolling on down hoops of white wisteria in the moon they came to the pillared circle of a rustic-temple, commanding a prospect on the town.

" There," she murmured smiling elfishly, and designating something, far below them,

through the moonmist, with her fan : " is
the column of Justice and," she laughed a
little, " of *Liberty* ! "

" And there," he pointed inconsequently,
" is *the Automobile Club* ! "

" And beyond it . . . The Convent of
the Flaming-Hood. . . ."

" And those blue revolving lights ; can
you see them, Rara ? "

" Yes, dear . . . what are *they*, Yousef ? "

" Those," he told her, contemplating her
beautiful white face against the dusky
bloom, " are the lights of the Café
Cleopatra ! "

" And what," she questioned, as they
sauntered on, pursued by all the sweet
perfumes of the night, " are those berried-
shrubs, that smell so passionately ? "

" I don't know," he said : " Kiss me,
Rara ! "

" No, no."

" Why not ? "

" Not now ! "

" Put your arm about me, dear."

" What a boy he is ! " she murmured,
gazing up into the starry clearness.

THE FLOWER BENEATH THE FOOT

Overhead a full moon, a moon of circumstance, rode high in the sky, defining phantasmally far off, the violet-farded hills beyond the town.

" To be out there among the silver bean-fields ! " he said.

" Yes, Yousef," she sighed, starting at a Triton's face among the trailing ivy on the castle wall. Beneath it, half concealed by water-flags, lay a miniature lake : as a rule now, nobody went near the lake at all, since the Queen had called it ' *appallingly smelly*,' so that, for rendezvous, it was quite ideal.

" Tell me, Yousef," she presently said, pausing to admire the beautiful shadow of an orange-tree on the path before them : " tell me, dear, when Life goes like that to one—what does one do ! ! "

He shrugged. " Usually nothing," he replied, the tip of his tongue (like the point of a blade) peeping out between his teeth.

" Ah, but isn't that being strong ? " she said half-audibly, fixing her eyes as though fascinated upon his lips.

" Why," he demanded with an engaging

smile that brought half-moons to his hollow cheeks : " What has the world been doing to Rara ? "

" At this instant, Yousef," she declared, " it brings her nothing but Joy ! "

" You're happy, my sweet, with me ? "

" No one knows, dearest, how much I love you."

" Kiss me, Rara," he said again.

" Bend, then," she answered, as the four quarters of the twelve strokes of midnight rang out leisurely from the castle clock.

" I've to go to the Ritz ! " he announced.

" And *I* should be going in."

Retracing reluctantly their steps they were soon in earshot of the ball, and their close farewells were made accompanied by selections from *The Blue Banana*.

She remained a few moments gazing as though entranced at his retreating figure, and would have, perhaps, run after him with some little capricious message, when she became aware of someone watching her from beneath the shadow of a garden vase.

Advancing steadily and with an air of

44

nonchalance, she recognised the delicate, sexless silhouette and slightly hunched shoulders of Olga Blumenghast, whose exotic attraction had aroused not a few heartburnings (and even feuds) among several of the grandes dames about the court.

Poised flatly against the vases' sculptured plinth, she would have scarcely have been discernible, but for the silver glitter of her gown.

" Olga ?   Are you faint ? "

" No ; only my slippers are *torture*."

" I'd advise you to change them, then ! "

" It's not altogether my feet, dear, that ache. . . ."

" Ah, I see," Mademoiselle de Nazianzi said, stooping enough to scan the stormy, soul-tossed eyes of her friend : " you're suffering, I suppose on account of Ann-Jules ? "

" He's such a gold-fish, Rara . . . any fingers that will throw him bread. . . ."

" And there's no doubt, I'm afraid, that lots do ! " Mademoiselle de Nazianzi answered lucidly, sinking down by her side.

45

" I would give all my soul to him, Rara
. . . my chances of heaven ! "

" Your chances, Olga——" Mademoiselle
de Nazianzi murmured, avoiding some bird-
droppings with her skirt.

" How I envy *the men*, Rara, in his
platoon ! "

" Take away his uniform, Olga, and what
does he become ? "

" Ah *what*—— ! "

" No. . . . Believe me, my dear, he's not
worth the trouble ! "

Mademoiselle Blumenghast clasped her
hands brilliantly across the nape of her
neck.

" I want to possess him at dawn, at
dawn," she broke out : " Beneath a sky
striped with green. . . ."

" Oh, Olga ! "

" And I never shall rest," she declared,
turning away on a languid heel, " until I
do."

Meditating upon the fever of Love,
Mademoiselle de Nazianzi directed her course
slowly towards her room. She lodged in
that part of the palace known as ' The

Bachelors' Wing,' where she had a delicious little suite just below the roof.

" If she loved him absolutely," she told herself, as she turned the handle of her door, " she would not care about the colour of the sky— ; even if it snowed, or hailed ! "

Depositing her fan upon the lid of an old wedding-chest that formed a couch, she smiled contentedly about her. It would be a wrench abandoning this little apartment that she had identified already with herself, when the day should come to leave it for others more spacious in the Keep. Although scarcely the size of a ship's cabin, it was amazing how many people one could receive together at a time merely by pushing the piano back against the wall, and wheeling the wedding-chest on to the stairs, and once no fewer than seventeen persons had sat down to a birthday *fête*, without being made too much to feel like herrings. In the so-called salon, divided from her bedroom by a folding lacquer screen, hung a few studies in oils executed by herself, and which, except to the initiated, or the naturally instinctive, looked sufficiently enigmatic against a wall-paper with a stealthy design.

Yes it would be a wrench to quit the little place, she reflected, as she began setting about her toilet for the night. It was agreeable going to bed late without anybody's aid, when one could pirouette interestingly before the mirror in the last stages of déshabille, and do a thousand (and one) things besides [1] that one might otherwise lack the courage for. But this evening being in no frivolous mood, she changed her ball-dress swiftly for a robe-de-chambre bordered deeply with ermins, that made her feel nearer somehow to Yousef, and helped her to realise, in its various facets, her position as future Queen.

" Queen ! " she breathed, trailing her fur flounces towards the window.

Already the blue revolving lights of the Café Cleopatra were growing paler with the dawn, and the moon had veered a little towards the Convent of the Flaming-Hood.

[1] Always a humiliating recollection with her in after years. *Vide*: ' Confessions.'

Ah . . . how often as a lay boarder there
had she gazed up towards the palace
wondering half-shrinkingly what life " in
the world " was like ; for there had been
a period indeed, when the impulse to take
the veil had been strong with her—more,
perhaps, to be near one of the nuns whom
she had *idolised* than from any more
immediate vocation.

She remained immersed in thoughts, her
introspectiveness fanned insensibly by the
floating zephyrs that spring with morning.
The slight sway-sway of the trees, the
awakening birds in the castle eaves, the
green-veined bougainvilleas that fringed
her sill—these thrilled her heart with joy.
All virginal in the early dawn what magic
the world possessed ! Slow speeding clouds
like knots of pink roses came blowing across
the sky, sailing away in titanic bouquets
above the town.

Just such a morning should be their
wedding-day ! she mused, beginning lightly
to apply the contents of a jar of Milk of
Almonds to her breast and arms. Ah,
before that Spina Christi lost its leaves,

or that swallow should migrate . . . that historic day would come !

Troops . . . hysteria . . . throngs. . . . The Blue Jesus packed to suffocation. . . . She could envisage it all.

And there would be a whole holiday in the Convent, she reflected falling drowsily at her bedside to her knees.

" Oh ! help me heaven," she prayed, " to be decorative and to do right ! Let me always look young, never more than sixteen or seventeen—at the *very* outside, and let Yousef love me—as much as I do him. And I thank you for creating such a darling, God (for he's a perfect dear), and I can't tell you how much I love him ; especially when he wags it ! I mean his tongue. . . . Bless all the sisters at the Flaming-Hood— above all Sister Ursula . . . and be sweet, besides, to old Jane. . . . Shew me the straight path ! And keep me ever free from the malicious scandal of the Court : Amen."

And her orisons (ending in a brief self-examination) over, Mademoiselle de Nazianzi climbed into bed.

III

IN the Salle de Prince or Cabinet
d'Antoine, above the Café Cleopatra,
Madame Wetme the wife of the pro-
prietor, sat perusing the Court gazettes.

It was not often that a *cabinet particulier*
like Antoine was disengaged at luncheon
time, being as a rule reserved many days
in advance, but it had been a ' funny '
season, as the saying went, and there was
the possibility that a party of late-risers
might look in yet (officers, or artistes
from the Halls), who had been passing a
night on the ' tiles.' But Madame Wetme
trusted not. It was pleasant to escape
every now and again from her lugubrious
back-drawing-room that only faced a
wall, or to peruse the early newspapers
without having first to wait for them.
And to-day precisely was the day for the
hebdomadal *causerie* in the *Jaw-waws'
Journal* on matters appertaining to society,

signed by that ever popular diarist " Eva Schnerb."

" Never," Madame Wetme read, " was a gathering more brilliant than that which I witnessed last night ! I stood in a corner of the Great ball room and literally *gasped* at the wealth of jewels. . . . Beauty and bravery abounded but no one, *I* thought, looked better than our most-gracious Queen, etc. . . . Among the supper-guests I saw their Excellencies Prince and Princess Paul de Pismiche,—the Princess impressed me as being *just* a trifle pale : she is by no means strong, and unhappily our nefarious climate does not agree with everybody ! Their Excellencies, Sir Somebody and Lady Something (Miss Ivy Something charming in cornflower *charmeuse* danced indefatigably all the evening, as did also one of the de Lambèse girls). The Count and Countess of Tolga—she all in blue furs and literally *ablaze* with gorgeous gems (I hear on excellent authority she is shortly relinquishing her post of Woman of the Bedchamber which she finds is really too arduous for her). The Duchess of Varna, looking veritably radiant (by the way where has she been ?) in the palest of pistachio-green mash-laks, which are all the rage at present.

"*Have you a Mashlak ?*

"Owing to the visit of King Jotifa and Queen Thleeanouhee, the Eastern mashlak is being worn by many of the smart women about the Court. I saw an example at the Opera the other night in silver and gold *lamé* that I thought too——"

Madame Wetme broke off to look up, as a waiter entered the room.

" Did Madame ring ? "

" No ! . . ."

" Then it must have been ' Ptolomy ' ! " the young man murmured, bustling out.

" I daresay. When will you know your bells ? " Madame Wetme retorted, returning with a headshake to the gazette : Her beloved Eva was full of information this week and breathlessly she read on :

" I saw Minnie, Lady Violetrock (whose daughter Sonia is being educated here) at the garden *fête* the other day, at the Château des Fleurs, looking chic as she

53

always does, in a combination of petunia and purple ninon raffling a donkey.

"I hear on the best authority that before the Court goes to the Summer-Palace later on, there will be at least *one* more Drawing-room. Applications, from those entitled to attend, should be made to the Lord Chamberlain as *soon* as possible."

One more Drawing-room—! the journal fell from Madame Wetme's hand.

"I'm getting on now," she reflected, "and if I'm not presented soon, I never will be. . . ."

She raised imploring eyes to the mural imagery—to the "Cleopatra couchant," to the "Arrival of Anthony," to the "Sphinx," to the "Temple of Ra," as though seeking inspiration : "Ah my God ! " she groaned.

But Madame Wetme's religion, her cruel God, was the *Chic* : The God Chic.

The sound of music from below reached her faintly. There was not a better orchestra (even at the Palace) than that which discoursed at the Café Cleopatra— and they played, the thought had some-times pleased her, the same identical tunes !

54

" Does it say when ? " she murmured, reopening the gazette. No : But it would be " before " the Court left. . . . And when would that be ?

" I have good grounds for believing," she continued to read : " that in order to meet his creditors, the Duke of Varna is selling a large portion of his country estate."

If it were true. . . . Madame Wetme's eyes rested in speculation on the Oleanders in the great flower-tubs before the Café, if it were true, why the Varnas must be desperate, and the Duchess ready to do anything. " Anything—for remuneration," she murmured, rising and going towards a table usually used for correspondence. And seating herself with a look of decision, she opened a leather writing-pad, full of crab-coloured ink-marked blotting paper.

In the fan-shaped mirror above the writing-table she could see herself in fancy, all veils and aigrettes, as she would be on " the day " when coiffed by Ernst.

" Among a bevy of charming débutantes, no one looked more striking than Madame Wetme, who was presented by the Duchess of Varna." Being a client of the house (with an unpaid bill) she could *dictate* to Eva. . . . But first, of course, she must secure the Duchess. And taking up her pen she wrote : " Madame Wetme would give the Duchess of Varna fifty thousand crowns to introduce her at Court." A trifle terse perhaps ? ? Madame Wetme considered. How if the Duchess should take offence. . . . It was just conceivable ! And besides, by specifying no fixed sum, she might be got for less.

"Something more mysterious, more delicate in style . . . ." Madame Wetme murmured with a sigh, beginning the letter anew :

" If the Duchess of Varna will call on Madame Wetme this afternoon, about five, and partake of a cup of tea, she will hear of something *to her advantage*."

Madame Wetme smiled : " That should get her ! " she reflected, and selecting an envelope, she directed it boldly to the Ritz. " Being hard up, she is sure to be there ! " she reasoned, as she left the room in quest of a page.

THE FLOWER BENEATH THE FOOT

The French maid of the Duchess of Varna was just putting on her mistress's shoes, in a private sitting-room at the Ritz, when Madame Wetme's letter arrived.

The pleasure of being in the capital once more, after a long spell of the country, had given her an appetite for her lunch and she was feeling braced after an excellent meal.

" I shall not be back, I expect, till late, Louison," she said to her maid, " and should anyone enquire where I am, I shall either be at the Palace, or at the Skating-Rink."

" Madame la Duchesse will not be going to her corsetier's ? "

" It depends if there's time. What did I do with my shopping-list ? " the Duchess replied, gathering up abstractedly a large, becoroneted vanity-case and a parasol. She had a gown of khaki and daffodil and a black tricorne hat trimmed with green. " Give me my other sunshade, the jade— and don't forget— : On me trouvera, Soit au Palais Royal, soit, au Palais de Glace ! " she enjoined sailing quickly out.

Leaving the Ritz by a side door, she

found herself in a quiet, shady street, bordering the Regina Gardens. Above a sky so blue, so clear, so luminous seemed to cry out : " Nothing matters ! Why worry ? Be sanguine ! Amuse yourself ! Nothing matters ! "

Traversing the gardens, her mind pre-occupied by Madame Wetme's note, the Duchess branched off into a busy thorough-fare, leading towards the Opera, in whose vicinity lay the city's principal shops. To learn of anything to one's advantage was, of course, always welcome, but there were various other claims upon her besides that afternoon, which she was unable, or loath to ignore—the palace, a *thé dansant* or two, and then her favourite rink . . . although the unfortunate part was, most of the rink instructors were still unpaid, and, on the last occasion she had hired a man to waltz with her, he had taken advantage of the fact by pressing her waist with greater freedom than she felt he need have done.

Turning into the Opera Square with its fine arcades, she paused, half furtively, before a Florist's shop. Only her solicitors and a few in the secret were aware that the premises known as *Haboubet of Egypt* were her own ; for fearful lest they might be occupied one day by sheriffs' officers, the little business venture had been kept the closest mystery. Lilies " from Karnak," Roses " from the Land of Punt " (all grown in the gardens of her country house, in the purlieus of the capital) found immediate and daily favour among amateurs of the choice. Indeed as her gardener frequently said, the demand for Roses from the Land of Punt, was more than he could possibly cope with without an extra man.

" I may as well run in and take whatever there's in the till," she reflected—" not that, I fear, there's much. . . ."

The superintendent, a slim Tunisian boy, was crouching pitcher-posture upon the floor, chanting languidly to himself, his head supported by an osier pannier lately arrived from " Punt."

" Up, Bachir ! " the Duchess upbraided. " Remember the fresh consignments perish, while you dream there and sing."

The young Tunisian smiled.

He worshipped the Duchess, and the song he was improvising as she entered, had been inspired by her. In it (had she known) he had led her by devious tender stages to his Father's fondouk at Tifilalet " on the blue Lake of Fetzara," where he was about to present her to the Cheikh, and the whole assembled village, as his chosen bride.

The Duchess considered him. He had a beautiful face spoiled by a bad complexion, which doubtless (the period of puberty passed) he would outgrow.

" Consignment him come not two minute," the youth replied.

" Ah Bachir ? Bachir ! "

" By the glorious Koran, I will swear it."

" Be careful not to shake those *Alexandrian Balls*," the Duchess peremptorily enjoined pointing towards some Guelder-roses—" or they'll fall before they're sold ! "

" No matter at all. They sold already ! An American lady this morning, she purchase all my Alexandrian-Balls ; two heavy bunch."

" Let me see your takings." . . .

With a smile of triumph, Bachir turned

THE FLOWER BENEATH THE FOOT

towards the till. He had the welfare of
the establishment at heart as well as his
own, and of an evening often he would flit,
garbed in his long gandourah, through the
chief Cafés and Dancings' of the city, a
vast pannier heaped high with flowers upon
his head, which he would dispose of to
dazzled clients for an often exorbitant sum.
But for these excursions of his (which ended
on occasion in adventure) he had received
no authority at all.

" Not so bad," the Duchess commented :
" And, as there's to be a Court again soon,
many orders for bouquets are sure to come
in ! "

" I call in outside hands to assist me :
I summon Ouardi ! He an Armenian boy.
Sympathetic. My friend. More attached
to him am I than a branch of Jessamine is
about a Vine."

" I suppose he's capable ? " the Duchess
murmured, pinning a green-ribbed orchid
to her dress.

" The garlands of Ouardi would make
even a jackal look bewitching ! "

" Ah : he has taste ? "

" I engage my friend.   Much work always in the month of Redjeb ! "

" Engage nobody," the Duchess answered as she left the shop, "until I come again."

Hailing one of the little shuttered cabs of the city in the square she directed the driver to drop her at the palace gates, and pursued by an obstreperous newsboy with an evening paper, yelling : " Chedorlahomor ! Sodom ! Extra Special ! " the cab clattered off at a languid trot. Under the plane-trees, near the Houses of Parliament, she was overtaken by the large easy-stepping horses of the Ambassadress of England, and acknowledged with a winning movement of the wrist, Lady Something's passing acceuil. It was yet not quite the correct hour for the Promenade, where beneath the great acacias Society liked best to ride or drive, but, notwithstanding, that zealous reporter of social deeds, the irrepressible Eva Schnerb, was already on the prowl and able with satisfaction to note : " I saw the Duchess of Varna early driving in the Park, all alone in a little one-horse shay, that really looked more elegant than any Delaunay-Belleville ! ''

Arriving before the palace gates, the Duchess perceived an array of empty carriages waiting in the drive, which made her apprehensive of a function. She had anticipated an intimate chat with the Queen alone, but this it seemed was not to be.

Following a youthful page with a *resigned* face, down a long black rug woven with green and violet flowers, who left her with a sigh (as if disappointed of a tip) in charge of a couple of giggling colleagues, and who, in turn, propelled her towards a band of sophisticated-looking footmen and grim officials, she was shewn at last into a vast white drawing-room whose ceiling formed a dome.

Knowing the Queen's interest in the Chedorlahomor Excavation Bill, a number of representative folk, such as the wives of certain Politicians or Diplomats, as well as a few of her own more immediate circle, had called to felicitate her upon its success. Parliament had declared itself willing to do the unlimited graceful by all those concerned, and this in a great measure was due to the brilliant wire pulling of the Queen.

She was looking singularly French in a gold helmet and a violet Vortniansky gown, and wore a rope of faultless pearls, clasped very high beneath the chin.

" I hope the Archbishop will bless the Excavators' tools ! " she was saying to the wife of the Premier, as the Duchess entered. " The *picks* at any rate. . . ."

That lady made no reply : In presence of royalty she would usually sit and smile at her knees, raising her eyes from time to time to throw, beneath her lashes, an ineffable expiring glance.

" God speed them safe home again ! " the Archduchess Elizabeth who was busy knitting said. An ardent philanthropist she had begun already making " comforts " for the men, as the nights in the East are cold. The most philanthropic perhaps of all the Royal Family, her hobby was designing, for the use of the public, sanitary, but artistic, places of Necessity on a novel system of ventilation. The King had consented to open (and it was expected appropriately) one of these in course of construction in the Opera Square.

"Amen," the Queen answered, signalling amiably to the Duchess of Varna, whose infrequent visits to court disposed her always to make a fuss of her.

But no fuss the Queen could make of the Duchess of Varna, could exceed that being made by Queen Thleeanouhee, in a far-off corner, of her Excellency, Lady Something. The sympathy, the *entente* indeed that had arisen between these two ladies was exercising considerably the minds of certain members of the diplomatic corps, although had anyone wished to eavesdrop, their conversation upon the whole must have been found to be anything but esoteric.

"What I want," Queen Thleeanouhee was saying, resting her hand confidentially on her Excellency's knee: "what I want is an English maid with Frenchified fingers—— Is there such a thing to be had?"

"But surely——" Lady Something smiled: for the servant-topic was one she felt at home on.

65

THE FLOWER BENEATH THE FOOT

" In Dateland, my dear, servant girls are
nothing but sluts."

" Life is like *that*, ma'am, I regret indeed,
to have to say : I once had a housemaid
who had lived with Sarah Bernhardt, and
oh, wasn't she a terror ! " Lady Something
declared, warding off a little black bat-
eared dog who was endeavouring to scramble
on to her lap.

" Teddywegs, Teddywegs ! " the Archduchess exclaimed jumping up and advancing to capture her pet : " He arrived from
London not later than this morning," she
said : " from the Princess Elsie of England."

" He looks like some special litter," Lady
Something remarked.

" How the dear girl loves animals ! "

" The rumour of her betrothal it seems
is quite without foundation ? "

" To my nephew : ah alas. . . ."

" Prince Yousef and she are of an equal
age ! "

" She is interested in Yousef I'm inclined
to believe ; but the worst of life is, nearly
everyone marches to a different tune," the
Archduchess replied.

" One hears of her nothing that isn't agreeable."

" Like her good mother, Queen Glory," the Archduchess said, " one feels, of course, she's all she should be."

Lady Something sighed.

" Yes . . . and even *more* ! " she murmured, letting fall a curtsy to King William who had entered. He had been lunching at the Headquarters of the Girl Guides, and wore the uniform of a general.

" What is the acme of nastiness ? " he paused of the English Ambassadress to enquire.

Lady Something turned paler than the white candytuft that is found on ruins. " Oh *la*, sir," she stammered, " how should I know ! "

The King looked the shrinking matron slowly up and down : " The supreme disgust——"

" Oh *la*, sir!" Lady Something stammered again.

But the King took pity on her evident confusion : " Tepid potatoes," he answered, " on a stone-cold plate."

The Ambassadress beamed.

" I trust the warmth of the girls, sir, compensated you for the coldness of the plates ? " she ventured.

" The inspection, in the main, was satisfactory ! Although I noticed that one or two of the guides, seemed inclined to lead astray," the King replied, regarding Teddywegs, who was inquisitively sniffing his spurs.

" He's strange yet to everything," the Archduchess commented.

" What's this—a new dog ? "

" From Princess Elsie. . . ."

" They say she's stupid, but I do not know that intellect is always a blessing ! " the King declared, drooping his eyes to his abdomen, with an air of pensive modesty.

" Poor child, she writes she is tied to the shore, so that I suppose she is unable to leave dear England."

" Tied to it ? "

" And bound till goodness knows."

" As was Andromeda ! " the King sententiously exclaimed. . . . " She would have little, or maybe nothing, to wear," he

68

clairvoyantly went on : " I see her standing shivering, waiting for Yousef. . . .
Chained by the leg, perhaps, exposed to the
howling winds." [1]

" Nonsense. She means to say she can't
get away yet on account of her engage-
ments : that's all."

" After Cowes-week," Lady Something
put in, " she is due to pay a round of visits
before joining her parents in the North."

" How I envy her," the Archduchess
sighed, " amid that entrancing scene. . . ."

Lady Something looked *attendrie*.

" Your royal highness is attached to
England ? " she asked.

" I fear I was never there. . . . But I
shall always remember I put my hair up
when I was twelve years old because of the
Prince of Wales."

" Oh ? And . . . which of the Georges ?"
Lady Something gasped.

" It's so long ago now that I really forget."

" And pray, ma'am, what was the point
of it ? "

The Archduchess chuckled :

[1] *Winds*, pronounced as we're told, "in poetry.'

" Why, so as to look eligible of course ! "
she replied, returning to her knitting.

Amid the general flutter following the
King's appearance, it was easy enough for
the Duchess of Varna to slip away. Knowing the palace inside out it was unnecessary
to make any fuss. Passing through a long
room, where a hundred holland-covered
chairs stood grouped, Congresswise, around
a vast table, she attained the Orangery,
that gave access to the drive. The mellay
of vehicles had considerably increased, and
the Duchess paused a moment to consider
which she should borrow, when recollecting
she wished to question one of the royal
gardeners on a little matter of mixing
manure, she decided to return through the
castle grounds instead. Taking a path
that descended between rhododendrons and
grim old cannons towards the town, she was
comparing the capriciousness of certain
bulbs to that of certain people, when she
heard her name called from behind, and
glancing round perceived the charming
silhouette of the Countess of Tolga.

" I couldn't stand it inside : Could you ? "

" My *dear*, what a honeymoon hat ! "

" It was made by me ! "

" Oh, Violet . . ." the Duchess murmured, her face taking on a look of wonder.

" Don't forget, dear, Sunday."

" Is it a party ? "

" I've asked Grim-lips and Ladybird, Hairy and Fluffy, Hardylegs and Bluewings, Spindleshanks, and Our Lady of Furs."

" Not Nanny-goat ? "

" Luckily . . ." the Countess replied, raising to her nose the heliotropes in her hand.

" Is he no better ? "

" You little know, dear, what it is to be all alone with him chez soi when he thinks and sneers into the woodwork."

" *Into the woodwork ?* "

He addresses the ceiling, the walls, the floor—me never ! "

" Dear dove."

" All I can I'm plastic."

" Can one be plastic ever enough, dear ? "

" Often but for Olga . . ." the Countess murmured considering a little rosy ladybird on her arm.

" I consider her ever so compelling, ever so wistful—" the Duchess of Varna averred.

" Sweet girl—! She's just my consolation."

" She reminds me, does she you, of that *Miss Hobart* in de Grammont's *Memoirs*."

" C'est une ame exquise ! "

" Well au revoir, dear : We shall meet again at the Princess Leucippe's later on," the duchess said, detecting her gardener in the offing.

By the time she had obtained her recipe and cajoled a few special shoots from various exotic plants, the sun had begun to decline. Emerging from the palace by a postern-gate, where lounged a sentry, she found herself almost directly beneath the great acacias on the Promenade. Under the lofty leafage of the trees, as usual towards this hour, society, in its varying grades had congregated to be gazed upon. Mounted on an eager-headed little horse his Weariness (who loved being seen) was plying up and down, while in his wake a " *screen artiste*," on an Arabian mare with powdered withers and eyes made up with kohl, was creating

a sensation. Every time she used her whip
the powder rose in clouds. Wending her
way through the throng the duchess recognised the rose-harnessed horses of
Countess Medusa Rappa—the Countess bolt
upright her head carried stiffly staring with
a pathetic expression of dead *joie-de-vie*
between her coachman's and footman's
waists. But the intention of calling at the
Café Cleopatra caused the duchess to hasten.
The possibility of learning something beneficial to herself was a lure not to be resisted.
Pausing to allow the marvellous blue automobile of Count Ann-Jules to pass (with
the dancer Kalpurnia inside), she crossed
the Avenue, where there seemed, on the
whole, to be fewer people. Here she remarked a little ahead of her the masculine
form of the Countess Yvorra, taking a quiet
stroll before *Salut* in the company of her
Confessor. In the street she usually walked
with her hands clasped behind her back,
huddled up like a statesman : " *Des choses
abominables ! . . . Des choses hors nature !* "
she was saying, in tones of evident relish,
as the duchess passed.

73

THE FLOWER BENEATH THE FOOT

Meanwhile Madame Wetme was seated anxiously by the samovar in her drawing-room. To receive the duchess, she had assumed a mashlak à la mode, whitened her face and rouged her ears, and set a small, but costly aigrette at an insinuating angle in the edifice of her hair. As the hour of Angelus approached, the tension of waiting grew more and more acute, and beneath the strain of expectation even the little iced-sugar cakes upon the tea-table looked green with worry.

Suppose, after all, she shouldn't come? Suppose she had already left? Suppose she were in prison? Only the other day a woman of the highest fashion, a leader of "society" with an *A*, had served six months as a consequence of her extravagance. . . .

In agitation Madame Wetme helped herself to a small glassful of *Cointreau*, (her favourite liqueur) when, feeling calmer for the consommation, she was moved to take a peep out of Antoine.

But nobody chic at all met her eye.

Between the oleanders upon the curb,

that rose up darkly against a flame-pink sky, two young men dressed " as Poets " were arguing and gesticulating freely over a bottle of beer. Near them, a sailor with a blue drooping collar and dusty boots (had he walked poor wretch to see his mother ?) was gazing stupidly at the large evening gnats that revolved like things bewitched about the café lamps. While below the window a lean soul in glasses, evidently an impresario, was loudly exclaiming: "London has robbed me of my throat, sir ! ! It has deprived me of my voice."

No, an " off " night certainly !

Through a slow, sun-flower of a door (that kept on revolving long after it had been pushed) a few military men bent on a game of billiards, or an early *fille de joie* (only the discreetest *des filles " serieuses "* were supposed to be admitted)—came and went.

" To-night they're fit for church," Madame Wetme complacently smiled as the door swung round again : " Navy-blue and silver-fox looks the goods," she reflected, " upon any occasion ! It suggests something sly—like a Nurse's uniform."

75

THE FLOWER BENEATH THE FOOT

" A lady in the drawing-room, Madame, desires to speak to you," a chasseur tunefully announced, and fingering nervously her aigrette Madame Wetme followed.

The Duchess of Varna was inspecting a portrait with her back to the door as her hostess entered.

" I see you're looking at my Murillo ! " Madame Wetme began.

" Oh. . . . Is it o-ri-gi-nal ? " the duchess drawled.

" No."

" I *thought* not."

" To judge by the Bankruptcy-sales of late (and it's curious how many there've been . . .) it would seem from the indifferent figure he makes, that he is no longer accounted chic," Madame Wetme observed as she drew towards the duchess a chair.

" I consider the chic to be such a very false religion ! . . ." the duchess said, accepting the seat which was offered her.

" Well, I come of an old Huguenot family myself ! "

" —— . . . ? "

" Ah my early home. . . . Now, I hear, it's nothing but a weed-crowned ruin."

The duchess considered the ivory cat handle of her parasol : " You wrote to me ? " she asked.

" Yes : about the coming court."

" About it ? "

" Every woman has her dream, duchess ! And mine's to be presented."

" The odd ambition ! " the duchess crooned.

" I admit we live in the valley.   Although *I* have a great sense of the hills ! " Madame Wetme declared demurely.

" Indeed ? "

" My husband you see . . . "

" . . . . "

" Ah ! well ! "

" Of course."

" If I'm not asked this time, I shall die of grief."

" Have you made the request before ? "

" I have attempted ! "

" Well ? "

" When the Lord Chamberlain refused

me, I shed tears of blood," Madame Wetme
wanly retailed.

" It would have been easier, no doubt,
in the late king's time ! "

Madame Wetme took a long sighing
breath.

" I only once saw him in my life," she
said, " and then he was standing against
a tree, in an attitude offensive to modesty."

" Tell me . . . as a public man, what
has your husband done——"

" His money helped to avert, I always
contend, the noisy misery of a War ! "

" He's open-handed ? "

" Ah . . . as you would find. . . ."

The duchess considered : " I *might*,"
she said, " get you cards for a State
concert. . . ."

" A State concert, duchess ? That's no
good to me ! "

" A drawing-room you know is a very
dull affair."

" I will liven it ! "

" Or an invitation perhaps to begin with
to one of the Embassies—the English for
instance might lead. . . ."

" Nowhere. . . . ! You can't depend on that : people have asked me to lunch, and left me to pay for them. . . . ! There is so much trickery in Society. . . ." Madame Wetme laughed.

The duchess smiled quizzically : " I forget if you know the Tolgas," she said.

" By ' name ' ! "

" The Countess is more about the throne at present than I."

" Possibly—but oh *you* who do *everything*, duchess ? " Madame Wetme entreated.

" I suppose there are things still one wouldn't do however——! " the duchess took offence.

" The Tolgas are so hard."

" You want a misfortune and they're sweet to you. Successful persons they're positively hateful to ! "

" These women of the Bedchamber are all alike so glorified. You would never credit they were Chambermaids at all ! I often smile to myself when I see one of them at a *première* at the Opera, gorged with pickings, and think that, most likely, but an hour before she was

stumbling along a corridor with a pailful
of slops ! "

" You're fond of music, Madame ? " the
duchess asked.

" It's my joy : I could go again and
again to *The Blue Banana* ! "

" I've not been."

" Pom-pom, pompity-pom ! We might
go one night, perhaps, together."

" . . ."

" Doudja Degdeg is always a draw,
although naturally now she is getting on ! "

" And I fear so must I "—the duchess
rose remarking.

" So soon ? "

"I'm only so sorry I can't stay longer——!"

" Then it's all decided," Madame Wetme
murmured archly as she pressed the bell.

" Oh I'd not say that."

" If I'm not asked remember this time,
I shall die with grief."

" To-night the duke and I are dining
with the Leucippes, and possibly . . ." the
duchess broke off to listen to the orchestra
in the café below, which was playing the
waltz-air from *Der Rosenkavalier*.

" They play well ! " she commented.

" People often tell me so."

" It must make one restless, dissatisfied, that yearning, yearning music continually at the door ? "

Madame Wetme sighed.

" It makes you often long," she said, " to begin your life again ! "

" Again ? "

" Really it's queer I came to yoke myself with a man so little fine. . . ."

" Still——— !   If he's open-handed," the duchess murmured as she left the room.

IV

ONE grey, unsettled morning (it was the first of June) the English Colony of Kairoulla [1] awoke in arms. It usually did when the Embassy entertained. But the omissions of the Ambassador, were, as old Mr Ladboyson the longest-established member of the colony declared, " not to be fathomed," and many of those overlooked declared they should go all the same. Why should Mrs Montgomery (who, when all was said and done, was nothing but a governess) be invited and not Mrs Barleymoon who was " nothing " (in the most distinguished sense of the word) at all ? Mrs Barleymoon's position, as a captain's widow with means, unquestionably came before Mrs Montgomery's, who drew a salary, and hadn't often an h.

Miss Grizel Hopkins, too—the cousin of an Earl, and Mrs Bedley the " Mother " of

[1] The Capital of Pisuerga.

the English Colony, both had been ignored. It was true Ann Bedley kept a circulating library and a tea-room combined and gave " Information " to tourists as well (a thing she had done these forty years), but was that a sufficient reason why she should be totally taboo ? *No*, in old Lord Clanlubber's time all had been made welcome, and there had been none of these heartburnings at all. Even the Irish coachman of the Archduchess was known to have been received—although it had been outside of course upon the lawn. Only gross carelessness, it was felt, on the part of those attachés could account for the extraordinary present neglect.

" I don't myself mind much," Mrs Bedley said, who was seated over a glass of morning milk and " a plate of fingers" in the *Circulating* end of the shop : " going out at night upsets me.   And the last time Dr Babcock was in he warned me not."

" What is the Embassy there for but to be hospitable ? " Mrs Barleymoon demanded from the summit of a ladder, from where she was choosing herself a book.

THE FLOWER BENEATH THE FOOT

" You're shewing your petticoat, dear—excuse me telling you," Mrs Bedley observed.

" When will you have something new, Mrs Bedley ? "

" Soon, dear . . . soon."

" It's always ' soon,' " Mrs Barleymoon complained.

" Are you looking for anything, Bessie, in particular ? " a girl, with loose blue eyes that did not seem quite firm in her head, and a literary face enquired.

" No, only something," Mrs Barleymoon replied, " I've not had before and before and before."

" By the way, Miss Hopkins," Mrs Bedley said, " I've to fine you for pouring tea over *My Stormy Past.*"

" It was coffee, Mrs Bedley—not tea."

" Never mind, dear, what it was the charge for a stain is the same as you know," Mrs Bedley remarked, turning to attend to Mrs Montgomery who, with his Lankiness, Prince Olaf, had entered the Library.

" Is it in ? " Mrs Montgomery mysteriously asked.

Mrs Bedley assumed her glasses.

" *Mmnops*," she replied, peering with an air of secretiveness in her private drawer where she would sometimes reserve or ' hold back ' a volume for a subscriber who happened to be in her special good graces.

" I've often said," Mrs Barleymoon from her ladder sarcastically let fall, " that Mrs Bedley has her pets ! "

" You are all my pets, my dear," Mrs Bedley softly cooed.

" Have you read *Men—my Delight*, Bessie ? " Miss Hopkins asked, " by Cora Velasquez."

" No ! "

" It's not perhaps a very . . . It's about two dark, and three fair, men," she added vaguely.

" Most women's novels seem to run off the rails before they reach the end, and I'm not very fond of them," Mrs Barleymoon said.

" And anyway, dear, it's out," Mrs Bedley asserted.

" *The Passing of Rose* I read the other day," Mrs Montgomery said, " and *so* enjoyed it."

"Isn't that one of Ronald Firbank's books?"

"No, dear, I don't think it is. But I never remember an author's name and I don't think it matters!"

"I suppose I'm getting squeamish! But this Ronald Firbank I can't take to at all. *Valmouth!* Was there ever a novel more coarse. I assure you I hadn't gone very far when I had to put it down."

"It's *out*," Mrs Bedley suavely said, "as well," she added, "as the rest of them."

"I once met him," Miss Hopkins said, dilating slightly the *retinæ* of her eyes: "He told me writing books was by no means easy!"

Mrs Barleymoon shrugged.

"Have you nothing more enthralling, Mrs Bedley," she persuasively asked, "tucked away?"

"Try *The Call of the Stage*, dear," Mrs Bedley suggested.

"You forget, Mrs Bedley," Mrs Barleymoon replied, regarding solemnly her *crêpe*.

"Or *Mary of the Manse*, dear."

THE FLOWER BENEATH THE FOOT

" I've read *Mary of the Manse* twice, Mrs Bedley—and I don't propose to read it again."

" . . . . ? "

" . . . . ! "

Mrs Bedley became abstruse.

" It's dreadful how many poets take to drink," she reflected.

A sentiment to which her subscribers unanimously assented.

" I'm taking *Men are Animals*, by the Hon. Mrs Victor Smythe, and *What Every Soldier Ought to Know*, Mrs Bedley," Miss Hopkins breathed.

" And I *The East is Whispering*," Mrs Barleymoon in hopeless tones affirmed.

" Robert Hitchinson! He's a good author."

" Do you think so? I feel his books are all written in hotels with the bed unmade at the back of the chair."

" And I daresay you're right, my dear."

" Well, Mrs Bedley, I must go—if I want to walk to my husband's grave," Mrs Barleymoon declared.

" Poor Bessie Barleymoon," Mrs Bedley

sighed, after Mrs Barleymoon and Miss Hopkins had gone : " I fear she frets ! "

" We all have our trials, Mrs Bedley."

" And some more than others."

" Court life, Mrs Bedley, it's a funny thing."

" It looks as though we may have an English Queen, Mrs Montgomery."

" I don't believe it ! "

" Most of the daily prints I see are devoting leaders to the little dog the Princess Elsie sent out the other day."

" Odious, ill-mannered, horrid little beast. . . ."

" It seems, dear, he ran from room to room looking for her until he came to the prince's door, where he just lay down and whined."

" And what does that prove, Mrs Bedley ? "

" I really don't know, Mrs Montgomery. But the press seemed to find it ' significant,' " Mrs Bedley replied as a Nun of the Flaming-Hood with a jolly face all gold with freckles entered the shop :

" Have you *Valmouth* by Ronald Firbank or *Inclinations* by the same author ? " she asked.

" Neither I'm sorry—both are out ! "

" Maladetta ✠ ✠ ✠ ✠ ! But I'll be passing soon again," the Sister answered as she twinklingly withdrew.

" You'd not think now by the look of her she had been at Girton ! " Mrs Bedley remarked.

" Once a Girton girl always a Girton girl, Mrs Bedley."

" It seems a curate drove her to it. . . ."

" I'm scarcely astonished. Looking back I remember the average curate at home as something between a eunuch and a snigger."

" Still, dear, I could never renounce my religion. As I said to the dear Chaplain only the other day (while he was having some tea), Oh, if only I were a man, I said ! Wouldn't I like to *denounce* the disgraceful goings on every Sabbath down the street at the church of the Blue Jesus."

" And I assure you it's positively *nothing*, Mrs Bedley, at the Jesus, to what it is at the church of St Mary the Fair ! I was at the wedding of one of the equerries lately, and never saw anything like it."

"It's about time there was an English wedding, in *my* opinion, Mrs Montgomery!"

"There's not been one in the Colony indeed for some time."

Mrs Bedley smiled undaunted.

"I trust I may be spared to dance before long at Dr and Mrs Babcock's!" she exclaimed.

"Kindly leave Cunnie out of it, Mrs Bedley," Mrs Montgomery begged.

"So it's Cunnie already you call him!"

"Dr Cuncliffe and I scarcely meet."

"People talk of the immense sameness of marriage, Mrs Montgomery; but all the same, my dear, a widow's not much to be envied."

"There are times, it's true, Mrs Bedley, when a woman feels she needs fostering; but it's a feeling she should try to fight against."

"Ah my dear, I never could resist *a mon*!" Mrs Bedley exclaimed.

Mrs Montgomery sighed.

"Once," she murmured meditatively, "men (those procurers of delights) engaged me utterly. . . . I was their *slave*. . . .

Now. . . . One does not burn one's fingers twice, Mrs Bedley.''

Mrs Bedley grew introspective.

" My poor husband sometimes would be a little frightening, a little fierce . . . at night, my dear, especially. Yet how often now I miss him ! ''

" You're better off as you are, Mrs Bedley, believe me," Mrs Montgomery declared, looking round for the little prince who was amusing himself on the library-steps.

" You must find him a handful to educate, my dear.''

" It will be a relief *indeed*, Mrs Bedley, when he goes to Eton ! ''

" I'm told so long as a boy is grounded . . .''

" His English accent is excellent, Mrs Bedley, and he shews quite a talent for languages," Mrs Montgomery assured.

" I'm delighted, I'm sure, to hear it ! ''

" Well, Mrs Bedley, I mustn't stand dawdling : I've to 'ave my 'air shampooed and waved for the Embassy party to-night you know ! '' And taking the little prince by the hand, the Royal Governess withdrew.

V

AMONG those attached to the Chedorlahomor expedition was a young
—if thirty-five be young—eccentric
Englishman from Wales, the Hon. 'Eddy'
Monteith, a son of Lord Intriguer. Attached
first to one thing and then another, without
ever being attached to any, his life had been
a gentle series of attachments all along.
But this new attachment was surely something better than a temporary secretaryship
to a minister, or " aiding " an ungrateful
general, or waiting in through draughts
(so affecting to the constitution) in the ante-
rooms of hard-worked royalty, in the purlieus of Pall Mall. Secured by the courtesy
of his ex-chief, Sir Somebody Something,
an old varsity friend of his father, the billet
of " surveyor and occasional help " to the
Chedorlahomorian excavation party had
been waywardly accepted by the Hon.
'Eddy' just as he had been upon the point

of attaching himself, to the terror of his relatives and the amusement of his friends, to a monastery of the Jesuit Order, as a likely candidate for the cowl.

Indeed he had already gone so far as to sit to an artist for his portrait in the habit of a monk, gazing ardently at what looked to be the Escurial itself, but in reality was nothing other than an " impression " from the kitchen garden of Intriguer Park. And now this sudden change, this call to the East instead. There had been no time, unfortunately, before setting out to sit again in the picturesque " sombrero " of an explorer, but a ready camera had performed miracles, and the relatives of the Hon. 'Eddy' were relieved to behold his smiling countenance in the illustrated-weeklies, pick in hand, or with one foot resting on his spade while examining a broken jar, with just below the various editors' comments : *To join the Expedition to Chedorlahomor—the Hon. ' Eddy ' Monteith, only son of Lord Intriguer ;* or, *Off to Chedorlahomor !* or, *Bon Voyage . . . !*

Yes, the temptation of the expedition

93

was not to be withstood, and for vows and
renunciations there was always time ! . . .
And now leaning idly on his window ledge
in a spare room of the Embassy, while his
man unpacked, he felt, as he surveyed the
distant dome of the Blue Jesus above the
dwarf-palm trees before the house, half-way
to the East already. He was suffering a
little in his dignity from the contretemps
of his reception, for having arrived at the
Embassy among a jobbed troop of serfs
engaged for the night, Lady Something had
at first mistaken him for one : " The cloak-
room will be in the Smoking-room ! " she
had said, and in spite of her laughing ex-
cuses and ample apologies, he could not
easily forget it. What was there in his
appearance that could conceivably recall a
cloak-room attendant—? *He* who had been
assured he had the profile of a " Rameses " !
And going to a mirror he scanned, with less
perhaps than his habitual contentment, the
light, liver-tinted hair, grey narrow eyes,
hollow cheeks, and pale mouth like a broken
moon. He was looking just a little fatigued
he fancied from his journey, and really, it

was all his hostess deserved, if he didn't go down.

" I have a headache, Mario," he told his man (a Neapolitan who had been attached to almost as many professions as his master). " I shall not leave my room ! Give me a kimono : I will take a bath."

Undressing slowly, he felt as the garments dropped away, he was acting properly in refraining from attending the soirée, and only hoped the lesson would not be " lost " on Lady Something, whom he feared must be incurably dense.

Lying amid the dissolving bath crystals while his man-servant deftly bathed him, he fell into a sort of coma, sweet as a religious trance.   Beneath the rhythmic sponge, perfumed with *Kiki*, he was St Sebastian, and as the water became cloudier and the crystals evaporated amid the steam, he was Teresa . . . and he would have been, most likely, the Blessed Virgin herself, but that the bath grew gradually cold.

" You're looking a little pale, sir, about the gills ! " the valet solicitously observed, as he gently dried him.

The Hon. 'Eddy' winced: "I forbid you ever to employ the word gill, Mario," he exclaimed. "It is inharmonious, and in English it jars; whatever it may do in Italian."

"Overtired, sir, was what I meant to say."

"Basta!" his master replied, with all the brilliant glibness of the Berlitz-school.

Swathed in towels, it was delicious to relax his powder-blanched limbs upon a comfy couch, while Mario went for dinner: "I don't care what it is! So long as it isn't—" (naming several dishes that he particularly abhorred, or might be "better," perhaps, without)—"And be sure, fool, not to come back without Champagne."

He could not choose but pray that the Ambassadress had nothing whatever to do with the Embassy cellar, for from what he had seen of her already, he had only a slight opinion of her discernment.

Really he might have been excused had he taken her to be the cook instead of the social representative of the Court of St James, and he was unable to repress a caustic smile on recollecting her appearance that afternoon, with her hat awry, crammed with *Maréchal Niel* roses, hot, and decoiffed, flourishing a pair of garden-gauntlets as she issued her commands. What a contrast to his own Mamma—" so different," . . . and his thoughts returned to Intriguer—" dear Intriguer, . . ." that if only to vex his father's ghost, he would one day turn into a Jesuit college ! The Confessional should be fitted in the paternal study, and engravings of the Inquisition, or the sweet faces of Lippi and Fra Angelico, replace the Agrarian certificates and tiresome trophies of the chase ; while the crack of the discipline in Lent would echo throughout the house ! How " useful " his friend Robbie Renard would have been ; but alas poor Robbie. He had passed through life at a rapid canter, having died at nineteen. . . .

Musingly he lit a cigarette.

Through the open window a bee droned in on the blue air of evening and closing his eyes he fell to considering whether the bee of one country would understand the

97

THE FLOWER BENEATH THE FOOT

remarks of that of another. The effect of the soil of a nation, had it consequences upon its Flora ? Were plants influenced at their roots ? People sometimes spoke (and especially ladies) of the language of flowers . . . the pollen therefore of an English rose would probably vary, not inconsiderably, from that of a French, and a bee born and bred at home (at *Intriguer* for instance) would be at a loss to understand (it clearly followed) the conversation of one born and bred, here, abroad. A bee's idiom varied then, as did man's ! And he wondered, this being proved the case, where the best bees' accents were generally acquired. . . .

Opening his eyes, he perceived his former school chum, Lionel Limpness—Lord Tiredstock's third (and perhaps most gifted) son, who was an honorary attaché at the Embassy, standing over him, his spare figure already arrayed in an evening suit.

" Sorry to hear you're off colour, Old Dear ! " he exclaimed, sinking down upon the couch beside his friend.

" I'm only a little shaken, Lionel . . . : have a cigarette."

" And so you're off to Chedorlahomor, Old Darling ? " Lord Tiredstock's third son said.

" I suppose so . . ." the only son of Lord Intriguer replied.

" Well, I wish I was going too ! "

" It would be charming, Lionel, of course to have you : but they might appoint you Vice-Consul at Sodom, or something ? "

" Why *Vice* ? Besides . . .! There's no consulate there yet," Lord Tiredstock's third son said, examining the objects upon the portable altar, draped in prelatial purple of his friend.

" Turn over, Old Dear, while I chastise you ! " he exclaimed, waving what looked to be a tortoiseshell lorgnon to which had been attached three threads of " cerulean " floss silk.

" Put it down, Lionel, and don't be absurd."

" Over we go. Come on."

" Really, Lionel."

" Penitence ! To thy knees, Sir ! "

And just as it seemed that the only son of Lord Intriguer was to be deprived of all his towels, the Ambassadress mercifully entered.

" *Poor* Mr Monteith ! " she exclaimed in tones of concern bustling forward with a tablespoon and a bottle containing physic, " *so* unfortunate. . . . Taken ill at the moment you arrive ! But Life is like that ! "

Clad in the flowing circumstance of an oyster satin ball dress, and all a-glitter like a Christmas tree (with jewels), her arrival perhaps saved her guest a " whipping."

" Had I known, Lady Something, I was going to be ill, I would have gone to the Ritz ! " the Hon. ' Eddy ' gasped.

" And you'd have been bitten all over ! " Lady Something replied.

" Bitten all over ? "

" The other evening we were dining at the Palace, and I heard the dear King say— but I oughtn't to talk and excite you——"

" By the way, Lady Something," Lord Tiredstock's third son asked : " what is the etiquette for the Queen of Dateland's eunuch ? "

" It's all according ; but you had better

THE FLOWER BENEATH THE FOOT

ask Sir Somebody, Mr Limpness," Lady
Something replied, glancing with interest
at the portable altar.

" I've done so, and he declared he'd be
jiggered ! "

" I recollect in Pera when we occupied
the Porte, they seemed (those of the old
Grand Vizier—oh what a good-looking man
he was—! such eyes—! and such a *way*
with him—! *Despot ! !*) only too thankful
to crouch in corners."

" Attention with that castor-oil . . . ! "

" It's not castor-oil ; it's a little decoc-
tion of my own,—aloes, gregory, a dash of
liquorice.   And the rest is buckthorn ! "

" Euh ! "

" It's not so bad, though it mayn't be
very nice. . . . Toss it off like a brave man,
Mr Monteith (nip his nostrils, Mr Limpness),
and while he takes it, I'll offer a silent prayer
for him at that duck of an altar," and as
good as her word, the Ambassadress made
towards it.

" You're altogether too kind," the Hon.
'Eddy' murmured seeking refuge in a book
—a volume of *Juvenalia* published for him

THE FLOWER BENEATH THE FOOT

by " Blackwood of Oxford," and becoming absorbed in its contents : " Ah Doris "— " Lines to Doris "—" Lines to Doris : written under the influence of wine, sun and fever " —" Ode to Swinburne "—" Sad Tamarisks " — " Rejection " — " Doigts Obscénes " — " They Call me *Lily*! "—" Land of Titian! Land of Verdi! Oh Italy! "—" I heard the Clock :

> I heard the clock strike seven,
> Seven strokes I heard it strike !
> His Lordship's gone to London
> And won't be back to-night."

He had written it at Intriguer, after a poignant domestic disagreement, his Papa, —the " his lordship " of the poem—had stayed away however considerably longer. . . . And here was a sweet thing suggested by an old Nursery Rhyme, " Loves, have you Heard " :

> " Loves, have you heard about the rabbits??
> They have such odd fantastic habits. . . .
> Oh, Children . . . ! I daren't disclose to You
> The licentious things *some* rabbits do."

THE FLOWER BENEATH THE FOOT

It had " come to him " quite suddenly out ferreting one day with the footman. . . .

But a loud crash as the portable altar collapsed beneath the weight of the Ambassadress aroused him unpleasantly from his thoughts.

" Horrid dangerous thing ! " she exclaimed as Lord Tiredstock's third son assisted her to rise from her " Silent " prayer : " I had no idea it wasn't solid ! But Life is like that . . ." she added somewhat wildly.

" Pity oh my God ! Deliver me ! " the Hon. 'Eddy' breathed, but the hour of *deliverance* it seemed was not just yet ; for at that instant the Hon. Mrs Chilleywater, the " literary " wife of the first attaché, thrust her head in at the door.

" How are you ? " she asked. " I thought perhaps I might find *Harold*. . . ."

" He's with Sir Somebody."

" Such mysteries ! " Lady Something said.

" This betrothal of Princess Elsie's is simply wearing him out," Mrs Chilleywater declared, sweeping the room with half-closed, expressionless eyes.

"It's a pity you can't pull the strings for us," Lady Something ventured : "I was saying so lately to Sir Somebody."

"I wish I could, dear Lady Something : I wouldn't mind wagering I'd soon bring it off!"

"Have you fixed up Grace Gillstow yet, Mrs Chilleywater?" Lord Tiredstock's third son asked.

"She shall marry Baldwin : but not before she has been seduced first by Barnaby. . . ."

"What are you talking about?" the Hon. 'Eddy' queried.

"Of Mrs Chilleywater's forthcoming book."

"Why should Barnaby get Grace—? Why not Tex!"

But Mrs Chilleywater refused to enter into reasons.

"She is looking for cowslips," she said, "and oh I've such a wonderful description of a field of cowslips. . . . They make quite a darling setting for a powerful scene of lust."

"So Grace loses her virtue! . . !" Lord Tiredstock's third son exclaimed.

" Even so she's far too good for Baldwin :
after the underhand shabby way he be-
haved to Charlotte, Kate, and Millicent ! "

"Life is like that, dear," the Ambassadress
blandly observed.

" It ought not to be, Lady Something ! "
Mrs Chilleywater looked vindictive.

Née Victoria Gellybore Frinton, and the
sole heir of Lord Seafairer of Sevenelms,
Kent, Mrs Harold Chilleywater, since her
marriage " for Love," had developed a disconcerting taste for fiction—a taste that
was regarded at the Foreign Office with
disapproving forbearance. . . . So far her
efforts (written under her maiden name in
full with her husband's as well appended)
had been confined to lurid studies of low
life (of which she knew nothing at all), but
the Hon. Harold Chilleywater had been
gently warned, that if he was not to remain
at Kairoulla until the close of his career, the
style of his wife must really grow less *virile*.

" I agree with V. G. F.," the Hon. Lionel
Limpness murmured fondling meditatively
his " Charlie Chaplin " moustache—" Life
ought not to be."

THE FLOWER BENEATH THE FOOT

" It's a mistake to bother oneself over matters that can't be remedied."

Mrs Chilleywater acquiesced : " You're right indeed, Lady Something," she said, " but I'm so sensitive. . . . I seem to *know* when I talk to a man, the colour of his braces . . . ! I say to myself : ' Yours are violet. . . .' ' Yours are blue. . . .' ' His are red. . . .' "

" I'll bet you anything, Mrs Chilleywater, you like, you won't guess what mine are," the Hon. Lionel Limpness said.

" I should say, Mr Limpness, that they were *multihued*—like Jacob's," Mrs Chilleywater replied, as she withdrew her head.

The Ambassadress prepared to follow :

" Come, Mr Limpness," she exclaimed, " we've exhausted the poor fellow quite enough — and besides, here comes his dinner."

" Open the champagne, Mario," his master commanded immediately they were alone.

" ' Small ' beer is all the butler would allow, sir."

" Damn the b . . . butler ! "

"What he calls a *demi-brune*, sir. In Naples we say *spumenti*!"

"To —— with it."

"Non é tanto amarro, sir; it's more sharp, as you'd say, than bitter. . . ."

". . . . . . !!!!!!"

And language *unmonastic* far into the night reigned supreme.

Standing beneath the portraits of King Geo and Queen Glory, Lady Something, behind a large sheaf of mauve malmaisons, was growing stiff. Already, for the most part, the guests were welcomed, and it was only the Archduchess now, who as usual was late, that kept their Excellencies lingering at the head of the stairs. Her Majesty Queen Thleeanouhee of the Land of Dates had just arrived, but seemed loath to leave the stairs, while her hostess, whom she addressed affectionately as her *dear gazelle*, remained upon them—" Let us go away by and by, my dear gazelle," she exclaimed with a primitive smile, "and remove our corsets and talk."

"Unhappily Pisuerga is not the East, ma'am!" Lady Something replied.

" Never mind, my dear ; we will introduce this innovation. . . ."

But the arrival of the Archduchess Elizabeth spared the Ambassadress from what might too easily have become an "incident."

In the beautiful chandeliered apartments several young couples were pirouetting to the inevitable waltz from the Blue Banana, but most of the guests seemed to prefer exploring the conservatories and Winter Garden, or elbowing their way into a little room where a new portrait of Princess Elsie had been discreetly placed. . . .

" One feels, of course, there *was* a sitting—; but still, it isn't like her ! " those that had seen her said.

" The artist has attributed to her at least the pale spent eyes of her father ! " the Duchess of Cavaljos remarked to her niece, who was standing quite silent against a rose-red curtain.

Mademoiselle de Nazianzi made no reply. Attaching not the faintest importance to the rumours afloat, still, she could not but feel, at times, a little heartshaken. . . .

The duchess plied her fan.

" She will become florid in time like her mother ! " she cheerfully predicted turning away just as the Archduchess approached herself to inspect the painting.

Swathed in furs, on account of a troublesome cough contracted paddling, she seemed nevertheless in charming spirits.

" Have you been to my new *Pipi* ? " she asked.

" Not yet——"

" Oh but you must ! "

" I'm told it's even finer than the one at the Railway Station. Ah, from musing too long on that Hellenic frieze, how often I've missed my train ! " the Duchess of Cavaljos murmured, with a little fat deep laugh.

" I have a heavenly idea for another— Yellow tiles with Thistles. . . ."

" Your Royal Highness never repeats herself ! "

" Nothing will satisfy me this time," the Archduchess declared, " but files of state-documents in all the dear little boxes : In secret, secrets ! " she added archly fixing her eyes on the assembly.

"It's positively pitiable," the Duchess of Cavaljos commented, "how the Countess of Tolga is losing her good-looks : She has the air to-night of a tired business-woman ! "

"She looks at other women as though she would inhale them," the Archduchess answered, throwing back her furs with a gesture of superb grace, in order to allow her robe to be admired by a lady who was scribbling busily away behind a door, with little nervous lifts of the head. For *noblesse oblige* the correspondent of the *Jaw-Waw*, the illustrious Eva Schnerb, was not to be denied.

"Among the many balls of a brilliant season," the diarist, with her accustomed fluency, wrote : "none surpassed that which I witnessed at the English Embassy last night. I sat in a corner of the Winter Garden and literally gorged myself upon the display of dazzling uniforms and jewels. The Ambassadress Lady Something was looking really regal in dawn-white draperies, holding a bouquet of the new mauve mal-maisons (which are all the vogue just now), but no one, *I* thought, looked better than the *Archduchess*, etc. . . . Helping the hostess, I noticed Mrs Harold Chilleywater, in an 'æsthetic' gown of flame-hued Kanitra silk edged with Armousky fur (to possess a dear woolly Armousk as a pet, is considered *chic* this season), while over her brain—an intellectual caprice, I wonder?—I saw a tinsel bow. . . . She is a daughter of the fortieth Lord Seafairer of Sevenelms-Park (so famous for its treasures) and is very artistic and literary having written several novels of English life under her maiden name of Victoria Gellybore-Frinton:—She inherits considerable cleverness *also* from her Mother. Dancing indefatigably (as she always does!) Miss Ivy Something seemed to be thoroughly enjoying her Father's ball: I hear on *excellent authority* there is no foundation in the story of her engagement to a certain young Englishman, said to be bound ere long for the ruins of Sodom and Gomorrah. Among the late arrivals were the Duke and Duchess of Varna—*she* all in golden tissues: they came together with Madame Wetme, who

THE FLOWER BENEATH THE FOOT

is one of the new hostesses of the season
you know, and they say has bought the
Duke of Varna's palatial town-house in
Samaden Square——"

"There," the Archduchess murmured,
drawing her wraps about her with a sneeze :
"she has said quite enough now I think
about my *toilette* ! "

But the illustrious Eva was in unusual
fettle, and only closed her notebook towards
Dawn, when the nib of her pen caught fire.

112

VI

AND suddenly the Angel of Death passed by and the brilliant season waned. In the Archduchess' bed-chamber, watching the antics of priests and doctors, he sat there unmoved. Propped high, by many bolsters, in a vast blue canopied bed, the Archduchess lay staring laconically at a diminutive model of a flight of steps, leading to what appeared to be intended, perhaps, as a hall of Attent, off which opened quite a lot of little doors, most of which bore the word: "Engaged." A doll, with a ruddy face, in charge, smiled indolently as she sat feigning knitting, suggesting vague "fleshly thoughts," whenever he looked up, in the Archduchess' spiritual adviser.

And the mind of the sinking woman, as her thoughts wandered, appeared to be tinged with "matter" too: "I recollect the first time I heard the *Blue-Danube* played!" she broke out: "it was at

Schonnbrunn — schönes Schonnbrunn — My
cousin Ludwig of Bavaria came—I wore—
the Emperor said——"

" If your royal highness would swallow
this ! " Dr Cuncliffe Babcock started forward with a glass.

" Trinquons, trinquons et vive l'amour !
Schneider sang that——"

" If your royal highness——"

" Ah my dear Vienna. Where's Teddywegs ? "

At the Archduchess' little escritoire at
the foot of the bed, her Dreaminess was
making ready a few private telegrams,
breaking without undue harshness the
melancholy news : " Poor Lizzie has ceased
articulating," she did not think she could
improve on it, and indeed had written it
several times in her most temperamental
hand, when the Archduchess had started
suddenly cackling about Vienna.

" *Ssssh*, Lizzie—I never can write when
people talk ! "

" I want Teddywegs."

" The Countess Yvorra took him for a
run round the courtyard."

" I think I must undertake a convenience
next for dogs. . . . It is disgraceful they
have not got one already, poor creatures,"
the Archduchess crooned accepting the
proffered glass.

" Yes, yes, dear," the Queen exclaimed
rising and crossing to the window.

The bitter odour of the oleander flowers
outside oppressed the breathless air and
filled the room as with a faint funereal
music. So still a day. Tending the
drooping sun-saturated flowers, a gardener
with long ivory arms alone seemed animate.

" Pull up your skirt, Marquise ! Pull it
up. . . . It's dragging, a little, in the water."

" *Judica me, Deus*," in imperious tones,
the priest by the bedside besought : " *et
discerne causam meum de gente non sancta.
Parce, Domine! Parce populo tuo—! ne
in aeternum irascaris nobis.*"

" A whale ! A whale ! "

" *Sustinuit anima mea in verbo ejus
speravit anima mea in Domino.*"

" Elsie ? " A look of wondrous happiness overspread the Archduchess' face—
She was wading — wading again among

the irises and rushes ; wading, her hand in Princess Elsie's hand, through a glittering golden sea, towards the wide horizon.

The plangent cry of a peacock, rose disquietingly from the garden.

" I'm nothing but nerves, doctor," her Dreaminess lamented, fidgeting with the crucifix that dangled at her neck upon a chain. *Ultra* feminine, she disliked that another—even *in extremis*—should absorb *all* the limelight.

" A change of scene, ma'am, would be probably beneficial," Dr Cuncliffe Babcock replied, eyeing askance the Countess of Tolga who unobtrusively entered :

" The couturiers attend your pleasure, ma'am," in impassive undertones she said : " to fit your mourning."

" Oh tell them the Queen is too tired to try on now," her Dreaminess answered repairing in agitation towards a glass.

" They would come here, ma'am," the Countess said, pointing persuasively to the little anteroom of the Archduchess, where two nuns of the Flaming-Hood were industriously telling their beads.

" ——I don't know why, but this glass refuses to flatter me ! "

" *Benedicamus Domino ! Ostende nobis Domine misericordiam tuam. Et salutare tuum da nobis !* "

" Well just a toque," the Queen sadly assented.

" *Indulgentiam absolutionem et remissionem peccatorum nostrorum tribuat nobis omnipotens et misericors Dominus.* "

" Guess who is at the Ritz, ma'am, this week ! " the Countess demurely murmured.

" Who is at the Ritz this week, I can't," the Queen replied.

" *Nobody !* "

" Why how so ? "

" The Ambassadress of England, it seems has alarmed the world away. I gather they mean to prosecute ! "

The Archduchess sighed.

" I want mauve sweet-peas," she listlessly said.

" Her spirit soars ; her thoughts are in the *Champs-Elysées*," the Countess exclaimed, withdrawing noiselessly to warn the milliners.

" Or in the garden," the Queen reflected, returning to the window. And she was standing there, her eyes fixed half wistfully upon the long ivory arms of the kneeling gardener, when the Angel of Death (who had sat unmoved throughout the day) arose.

It was decided to fix a period of mourning of fourteen days for the late Archduchess.

VII

SWANS and sunlight. A little fishing boat with coral sails. A lake all grey and green. Beatitude intense. Consummate calm. It was nice to be at the Summer-Palace after all.

"The way the air will catch your cheek and make a rose of it," the Countess of Tolga breathed. And as none of the company heeded her: "How sweetly the air takes one's cheek," she sighed again.

The post-prandial exercise of the members of the Court through the palace grounds was almost an institution.

The first half of the mourning prescribed, had as yet not run its course, but the tongues of the Queen's ladies had long since made an end of it.

"I hate dancing with a fat man," Mademoiselle de Nazianzi was saying: "for if you dance at all near him, his stomach hits you, while if you pull away, you catch either the scent of his breath or the hair of his beard."

"But, you innocent baby, *all* big men haven't beards," Countess Medusa Rappa remarked.

"Haven't they? Never mind. Everything's so beautiful," the young girl inconsequently exclaimed : "Look at that Thistle ! and that Bee ! O, you darling ! "

"Ah, how one's face unbends in gardens ! " the Countess of Tolga said, regarding the scene before her, with a faraway pensive glance.

Along the lake's shore, sheltered from the winds by a ring of wooded hills, shewed many a proud retreat, mirroring its marble terraces to the waveless waters of the lake.

Beneath a twin-peaked crag (known locally as the White Mountain whose slopes frequently would burst forth into patches of garlic that from the valley resembled snow) nestled the Villa Clement, rented each season by the Ambassador of the Court of St James, while half-screened by conifers and rhododendrons, and in the lake itself, was St Helena—the home and place of retirement of a "fallen" minister of the Crown.

Countess Medusa Rappa cocked her sunshade; "Whose boat is that," she asked, "with the azure oars?"

"It looks nothing but a pea-pod!" the Countess of Tolga declared.

"It belongs to a darling, with delicious lips and eyes like brown chestnuts," Mademoiselle de Lambèse informed.

"Ah!. . . Ah!. . . Ah!. . . Ah!. . ." her colleagues crooned.

"A sailor?"

The Queen's maid nodded: "There's a partner, though," she added, "A blue-eyed, gashed-cheeked angel. . . ."

Mademoiselle de Nazianzi looked away.

"I love the lake with the white wandering ships," she sentimentally stated, descrying in the distance the prince.

It was usually towards this time, the hour of the siesta, that the lovers would meet and taste their happiness, but, to-day, it seemed ordained otherwise.

Before the heir apparent had determined whether to advance or retreat, his father and mother were upon him, attended by two dowagers newly lunched.

"The song of the pilgrim women, how it haunts me," one of the dowagers was holding forth : "I could never tire of that beautiful, beautiful music ! Never tire of it. Ne-ver. . . ."

"Ta, ta, ta, ta," the Queen vociferated girlishly, slipping her arm affectionately through that of her son's.

"How spent you look, my boy. . . . Those eyes . . ."

His Weariness grimaced.

"They've just been rubbing in Elsie!" he said.

"Who ? "

"'Vasleine' and 'Nanny-goat'!"

"Well ? "

"Nothing will shake me."

"What are your objections ? "

"She's so extraordinarily uninteresting ! "

"Oh Yousef!" his mother faltered : "*Do you wish to break my heart ?* "

"We had always thought you too lacking in initiative," King William said (tucking a few long hairs back into his nose) " to marry against our wishes."

" They say she walks too wonderfully," the Queen courageously pursued.

" What ?   Well ? "

" Yes."

" Thank God for it."

" And can handle a horse as few others can ! "

Prince Yousef closed his eyes.

He had not forgotten how as an undergraduate in England he had come upon the princess once while out with the hounds. And it was only by a consummate effort that he was able to efface the sinister impression she had made—her lank hair falling beneath a man's felt-hat, her habit skirt torn to tatters, her full cheeks smeared in blood ; the blood, so it seemed, of her " first " fox.

A shudder seized him.

" No, nothing can possibly shake me," he murmured again.

With a detached, cold face, the Queen paused to inhale a rose.

(Oh you gardens of Palaces . . . !   How

often have you witnessed agitation and disappointment ? You smooth, adorned paths . . . ! How often have you known the extremes of care . . . ?)

" It would be better to do away I think next year with that bed of cinerarias altogether," the Queen of Pisuerga remarked, " since persons won't go round it."

Traversing the flower plat now, with the air of a black-beetle with a purpose, was the Countess Yvorra.

" We had supposed you higher-principled, Countess," her sovereign admonished.

The Countess slightly flushed.

" I'm looking for groundsel for my birds, Sire," she said—" for my little dickies ! "

" We understand your boudoir is a sort of menagerie," His Majesty affirmed.

The Countess tittered.

" Animals love me," she archly professed. " Birds perch on my breast if only I wave. . . . The other day a sweet red robin came and stayed for hours . . . ! "

" The Court looks to you to set a high example," the Queen declared, focusing quizzically a marble shape of Leda green with moss, for whose time-corroded plinth the late Archduchess' toy-terrier was just then shewing a certain contempt.

The Countess' long, slightly pulpy fingers strayed nervously towards the rosary at her thigh.

" With your majesty's consent," she said, " I propose a campaign to the Island."

" What ?   And beard the Count ? "

" The salvation of one so fallen, in my estimation should be worth hereafter (at the present rate of exchange, but the values vary) . . . a Plenary perpetual-indulgence : I therefore," the Countess said, with an upward fleeting glance (and doubtless guile-less of intention of irony), " feel it my *duty* to do what I can."

" I trust you will take a bodyguard when you go to St Helena ? "

" And pray tell Count Cabinet from us," the King looked implacable : " we forbid him to serenade the Court this year ! or to throw himself into the Lake again or to make himself a nuisance ! "

" He was over early this morning, Willie," the Queen retailed : " I saw him

from a window. Fishing, or feigning to!
And with white kid gloves, and a red
carnation."

"Let us catch him stepping ashore!"
the King displayed displeasure.

"And as usual the same mignon youth
had the charge of the tiller."

"I could tell a singular story of that
young man," the Countess said: "for he
was once a choir-boy at the Blue Jesus.
But, perhaps, I would do better to spare
your ears. . . ."

"You would do better, a good deal, to
spare my cinerarias," her Dreaminess
murmured, sauntering slowly on.

Sun so bright, trees so green, it was a
perfect day. Through the glittering fronds
of the palms shone the lake like a floor of
silver glass strewn with white sails.

"It's odd," the King observed, giving the
dog Teddywegs a sly prod with his cane,
"how he follows Yousef."

"He seems to know!" the Queen
replied.

A remark that so annoyed the Prince
that he curtly left the garden.

VIII

BUT this melancholy period of *crêpe*, a time of idle secrets, and unbosomings, was to prove fatal to the happiness of Mademoiselle de Nazianzi. She now heard she was not the first in the Prince's life, and that most of the Queen's maids, indeed, had had identical experiences with her own. She furthermore learned, amid ripples of laughter, of her lover's relations with the Marquesa Pizzi-Parma and of his light dealings with the dancer April Flowers, a negress (to what depths ??) at a time when he was enjoying the waxen favours of the wife of his Magnificence, the Master of the Horse.

Chilled to the point of numbness, the mortified girl had scarcely winced, and when on repairing to her room a little later, she had found his Weariness wandering in the corridor on the chance of a surreptitious kiss, she had bolted past him without look, or word, and sharply closed her door.

THE FLOWER BENEATH THE FOOT

The Court had returned to colours when she opened it again, and such had been the trend of her meditations, that her initial steps were directed, with deliberate austerity, towards the basilica of the Palace.

Except for the Countess Yvorra, with an *écharpe de décence* drawn over her hair, there was no one in it.

" I thank Thee God for this *escape*," she murmured falling to her knees before the silver branches of a cross : " It is terrible ; for I did so love him....................
....
....
........and oh how could he ever with *a negress* ? ....
....
........Pho ....
............I fear this complete upset has considerably aged me..................
........But to Three I cling............
....
....
Preserve me at all times from the toils of the wicked, and forgive him, as *I* hope to forgive him soon." Then kindling several

candles with a lingering hand, she shaped her course towards the Kennels, called Teddywegs to her and started, with an aching heart, for a walk.

It was a day of heavy somnolence. Skirting the Rosery where gardeners with their slowly moving rakes were tending the sandy paths, she chose a neglected footway that descended towards the lake. Indifferent to the vivacity of Teddywegs, who would race on a little before her, then wait with leonine accouchments of head until she had almost reached him, when he would prick an ear and spring forward with a yap of exhortation, she proceeded leisurely, and with many a pause, wrapped in her own mournful thoughts.

Alack! Among the court circle there was no one to whom in her disillusion she could look for solace, and her spirit yearned for Sister Ursula, and the Convent of the Flaming-Hood.

Wending her way amid the tall trees, she felt she had never cared for Yousef as she had for Ursula . . . and broodingly, in order to ease her heart, she began comparing the two together as she walked along.

THE FLOWER BENEATH THE FOOT

After all what had he ever said that was not either commonplace or foolish? Whereas Sister Ursula's talk was invariably pointed; and often indeed so delicately, that words seemed almost too crude a medium to convey her ethereal meanings, and she would move her evocative hands, and flash her aura, and it was no fault of hers if you hadn't a peep of the beyond. And the infinite tenderness of her least caress. Yousef's lips had seldom conveyed to hers the spell of Ursula's; and once indeed lately, when he had kissed her, there had been an unsavoury aroma of tobacco and *charcuterie*, which, to deal with, had required both tact and courage. . . . Ah dear Hood! What harmony life had held within. Unscrupulous and deceiving men might lurk around its doors (they often did) coveting the chaste, but Old Jane, the porteress, would open to no man beyond the merest crack. And how right they were the nuns in their mistrust of man! Sister Ursula one day had declared, in uplifted mood, that "marriage was obscene." Was it—? . . . ?? . . . Perhaps it might be—! How appalling if it was!

THE FLOWER BENEATH THE FOOT

She had reached the lake.

Beneath a sky as white as platinum it lay, pearly, dove-like, scintillating capriciously where a heat-shrouded sun kindled its torpid waters into fleeting diamonds. A convulsive breeze strayed gratefully from the opposite shore, descending from the hills that rose up all veiled, and without detail, against the brilliant whiteness of the morning.

Sinking down upon the shingle by an upturned boat, she heaved a brief sigh, and drawing from her vanity-case the last epistles of the Prince, she began methodically to arrange them in their proper sequence.

(*1*) "What is the matter with my Dearest Girl ? "

(*2*) " My own tender little Lita, I do not understand—"

(*3*) " Darling, what's this—? "

(*4*) " Beloved one, I swear—"

(*5*) " Your cruel silence—"

If published in a dainty brochure format about the time of his Coronation, they ought to realise no contemptible sum, and the proceeds might go to Charity, she reflected, thrusting them back again carefully into the bag.

131

Then, finding the shingle too hard through her thin gown to remain seated long, she got up, and ran a mournful race with Teddy-wegs along the shore.

Not far along the lake was the "village," with the Hôtel d'Angleterre et du Lac, its stucco, belettered-walls professing: "Garages, Afternoon Tea, Modern Comfort!" Flitting by this, and the unpretentious pier (where long, blonde fishing-nets lay drying in the sun), it was a relief to reach the remoter plage beyond.

Along the banks stretched vast brown carpets of corn and rye, broken by an occasional olive-garth, beneath whose sparse shade the heavy-eyed oxen blinked and whisked their tails, under the attacks of the water-gnats that were swarming around.

Musing on Negresses — and Can-Can dancers in particular—she strolled along a strand all littered with shells and little jewel-like stones.

The sun shone down more fiercely now, and soon, for freshness sake, she was obliged to take to the fields.

Passing among the silver drooping olives,

relieved here and there by a stone-pine,
or slender cypress-tree eternally green, she
sauntered on, often lured aside to pluck
the radiant wild-flowers by the way. On
the banks the pinkest cyclamens were in
bloom, and cornflowers of the hue of paradise, and fine-stemmed poppies flecked
with pink.

" Pho ! A Negress . . ." she murmured,
following the flight of some waterfowl
towards the opposite shore.

The mists had fallen from the hills,
revealing old woods wrapped in the blue
doom of Summer.

Beyond those glowing heights, towards
this hour, the nuns, each in her cool,
shuttered, cell, would be immersed in
noontide prayer.

" Ursula—for thee ! " she sighed, proffer-
ing her bouquet in the direction of the town.

A loud splash . . . the sight of a pair of delicate legs (mocking the Law's requirements
under the Modesty Act as relating to bathers).
. . . Mademoiselle de Nazianzi turned and
fled. She had recognised *the Prince.*[1]

[1] The recollection of this was never quite forgotten.

IX

AND in this difficult time of spiritual
distress, made more trying perhaps
because of the blazing midsummer
days, and long, pent feverish nights,
Mademoiselle de Nazianzi turned in her
tribulation towards religion.

The Ecclesiastical set at Court, composed
of some six, or so, ex-Circes, under the command of the Countess Yvorra, were only
too ready to welcome her, and invitations
to meet Monsignor this, or " Father " that,
who constantly were being *coaxed* from their
musty sacristies and wan-faced acolytes in
the capital, in order that they might offici-
ate at Masses, Confessions and Breakfast-
parties *à la fourchette*, were lavished daily
upon the bewildered girl.

Messages, and hasty informal lightly-
pencilled notes, too, would frequently reach
her ; such as : " I shall be pouring out
cocoa after dinner in bed. Bring your

biscuits and join me ! " . . . or a rat-a-
tat from a round-eyed page and : " The
Countess' comp'ts and she'd take it a
Favour if you can make a ' Station ' with her
in chapel later on," or : " The Marchioness
will be birched to-morrow, and *not* to-day."

O, the charm, the flavour of the religious
world ! Where match it for interest or
variety !

An emotion approaching sympathy had
arisen, perhaps a trifle incongruously, between the injured girl and the Countess
Yvorra, and before long, to the amusement
of the sceptical element of the Court, the
Countess and her Confessor, Father Nostradamus, might often be observed in her
society.

" I need a cage-companion, Father, for
my little bird," the Countess one evening
said, as they were ambling, all the three of
them before Office up and down the perfectly tended paths : " ought it to be of the
same species and sex, or does it matter ? For
as I said to myself just now (while listening
to a thrush), *All* birds are His creatures."

The priest discreetly coughed.

"Your question requires reflection," he said : "What is the bird?"

"A hen canary!—and with a voice, Father! Talk of soul!!"

"H—m . . . a thrush and a canary, I would not myself advise."

Mademoiselle de Nazianzi tittered.

"Why not let it go?" she asked, turning her eyes towards the window-panes of the palace, that glanced like rows of beaten-gold in the evening sun.

"A hawk might peck it!" the Countess returned, looking up as if for one, into a sky as imaginative, and as dazzling as Shelley poetry.

"Even the Court," Father Nostradamus ejaculated wryly, "will peck at times."

The Countess' shoulder-blades stiffened.

"After over thirty years," she said, "I find Court-life *pathetic*. . . ."

"Pathetic?"

"Tragically pathetic. . . ."

Mademoiselle de Nazianzi considered wistfully the wayward outline of the hills.

"I would like to escape from it all for a while," she said, "and travel."

" I must hunt you out a pamphlet, by
and by, dear child, on the ' Dangers of
Wanderlust.' "

" The Great Wall of China and the Bay
of Naples ! It seems so frightful never to
have seen them ! "

" I have never seen the Great Wall,
either," the Countess said, " and I don't
suppose, my dear, I ever shall ; though I
once did spend a fortnight in Italy."

" Tell me about it."

The Countess became reminiscent.

" In Venice," she said, " the indecent
movements of the Gondolieri quite affected
my health, and, in consequence, I fell a prey
to a sharp nervous fever. My temperature
rose and it rose, ah, yes . . . until I became
quite ill. At last I said to my maid (she
was an English girl from *Wales*, and almost
equally as sensitive as me) : ' Pack. . . .
Away ! ' And we left in haste for Florence.
Ah, and Florence, too, I regret to say I
found very far from what it ought to have
been ! ! ! I had a window giving on the
Arno, and so I could *observe*. . . . I used to
see some curious sights ! I would not care

to scathe your ears, my Innocent, by an inventory of one half of the wantonness that went on ; enough to say the tone of the place forced me to fly to Rome, where beneath the shadow of dear St Peter's I grew gradually less distressed."

"Still, I should like, all the same, to travel ! " Mademoiselle de Nazianzi exclaimed, with a sad little snatch of a smile.

"We will ask the opinion of Father Geordie Picpus, when he comes again."

"It would be more fitting," Father Nostradamus murmured (professional rivalry leaping to his eye), " if Father Picpus kept himself free of the limelight a trifle more ! "

"Often I fear our committees would be corvés without him. . . ."

"Tchut."

"He is very popular . . . too popular, perhaps . . ." the Countess admitted. " I remember on one occasion in the Blue Jesus, witnessing the Duchess of Quaranta and Madame Ferdinand Fishbacher, fight like wild cats as to which should gain his ear—(any girl might envy Father Geordie his ear)—at Confession next. The odds seemed fairly equal, until the Duchess gave the Fishbacher-woman, such a violent push —(well down from behind, in the crick of the joints)—that she overturned The Confessional Box, with Father Picpus within : and when we scared ladies, standing by, had succeeded in dragging him out, he was too shaken, naturally as you can gather, to absolve anyone else *that* day."

" He has been the object of so many unseemly incidents, that one can scarcely recall them all," Father Nostradamus exclaimed, stooping to pick up a dropped pocket-handkerchief with " remembrance " knots tied to three of the corners.

" Alas. . . . Court life is not uplifting," the Countess said again, contemplating her muff of *self-made* lace, with a half-vexed forehead. What that muff contained was a constant problem for conjecture ; but it was believed by more than one of the maids-in-waiting to harbour " goody " books and martyrs' bones.

" By generous deeds and Brotherly love," Father Nostradamus exclaimed, " we should endeavour to rise above it ! "

With the deftness of a virtuoso, the Countess seized, and crushed with her muff, a pale-winged passing gnat.

" Before Life," she murmured, " that saddest thing of all, was thrust upon us, I believe I was an angel. . . ."

Father Nostradamus passed a musing hand aross his brow.

" It may be," he replied, " and it very well may be," he went on, "that our ante-nativity was a little more brilliant, a little more *h—m* . . . ; and there is nothing un-orthodox in thinking so."

" O what did I do then to lose my wings ? ? What did I ever say to Them ? ! Father, Father. How did I annoy God ? Why did He put me here ? "

" My dear child, you ask me things I do not know ; but it may be you were the in-strument appointed above to lead back to Him our neighbour yonder," Father Nos-tradamus answered, pointing with his breviary in the direction of St Helena.

" Never speak to me of that wretched old man."

For despite the ablest tactics, the most

diplomatic angling, Count Cabinet had refused to rally.

" We followed the sails of your skiff to-day," Mademoiselle de Nazianzi sighed, " until the hazes hid them ! "

" I had a lilac passage."

" You delivered the books ? "

The Countess shrugged.

" I shall never forget this afternoon," she said. " He was sitting in the window over a decanter of wine when I floated down upon him ; but no sooner did he see me, than he gave a sound, like a bleat of a goat, and disappeared : I was determined however to call ! There is no bell to the villa, but two bronze door-knockers, well out of reach, are attached to the front-door. These with the ferrule of my parasol I tossed and I rattled, until an adolescent, with Bougainvillea at his ear, came and looked out with an insolent grin, and I recognised Peter Passer from the Blue Jesus grown quite fat."

" Eh mon Dieu ! " Father Nostradamus half-audibly sighed.

" Eh mon Dieu . . ." Mademoiselle de

Nazianzi echoed, her gaze roving over the palace, whose long window-panes in the setting sun gleamed like sumptuous tissues.

" So that," the Countess added, " I hardly propose to venture again."

"What a site for a Calvary!" Father Nostradamus replied, indicating with a detached and pensive air the cleft in the White Mountain's distant peaks.

" I adore the light the hills take on when the sun drops down," Mademoiselle de Nazianzi declared.

" It must be close on *Salut*. . . ."

It was beneath the dark colonnades by the Court Chapel door that they received the news from the lips of a pair of vivacious dowagers that the Prince was to leave the Summer-Palace on the morrow to attend " the Manœuvres," after which it was expected his Royal Highness would proceed " *to England*."

X

AND meanwhile the representatives of the Court of St James were enjoying the revivifying country air and outdoor-life of the Villa Clement. It was almost exquisite how rapidly the casual mode of existence adopted during the summer villeggiatura by their Excellencies, drew themselves and their personnel together, until soon they were as united and as *sans gêne* as the proverbial family party. No mother, in the " acclimatization " period, could have dosed her offspring more assiduously than did her Excellency the attachés in her charge ; flavouring her little inventions frequently with rum or gin until they resembled cocktails. But it was Sir Somebody himself if anyone that required a tonic. Lady Something's pending litigation, involving as it did the crown, was fretting the Ambassador more than he cared to admit, and the Hon. Mrs Chilleywater, ever alert, told " Harold " that the injudicious chatter of the Ambassadress (who even now notwithstanding her writ, would say to every other visitor that came to the villa : " Have you heard about the Ritz ? ? The other night we were dining at the Palace, and I heard the King," *etc.*) was wearing their old Chief out.

And so through the agreeable vacation life there twitched the grim vein of tension.

One day disturbed by her daughter's persistent trilling of the latest coster song *When I sees 'im I topple giddy*, Lady Something gathered up her morning letters and stepped out upon the lawn.

Oh so formal, oh so slender towered the Cypress-trees against the rose-farded hills and diamantine waters of the lake. The first hint of Autumn was in the air ; and over the gravel paths, and in the basins of the fountains, a few shed leaves lay hectically strewn already.

Besides an under-stamped missive, with a foreign postmark, from her Majesty the Queen of the Land of Dates beginning " My dear Gazel," there was a line from the eloquent, and moderately-victorious, young

barrister, engaged in the approaching suit
with the Ritz: He had spared himself no
pains he assured his client in preparing
the defence, which was he said to be *the
respectability of Claridge's*.

" Why bring in Claridge's? . . . ? " the
Ambassadress murmured, prodding with the
tip of her shoe a decaying tortoiseshell leaf ;
" but anyway," she reflected, " I'm glad
the proceedings fall in winter, as I always
look well in furs."

And mentally she was wrapped in leopard
skins and gazing round the crowded court
saluting with a bunch of violets an acquaintance here and there, as her eyes
fell on Mrs Chilleywater seated in the act
of composition beneath a cedar-tree.

Mrs Chilleywater extended a painful smile
of welcome which revealed her pointed
teeth and pale-hued gums, repressing,
simultaneously, an almost irresistible inclination to murder.

" What ! . . . Another writ ? " she
suavely asked.

" No, dear ; but these legal men *will*
write. . . ."

" I love your defender. He has an air of d'Alembert sympathetic soul."

" He proposes pleading Claridge's."

" Claridge's ? "

" Its respectability."

" Are hotels ever respectable,—I ask you. Though, possibly, the horridest are."

" Aren't they all horrid ! "

"*Natürlich;* but do you know those cheap hotels where the guests are treated like naughty children ? "

" No. I must confess I don't," the Ambassadress laughed.

" Ah, there you are. . . ."

Lady Something considered a moment a distant gardener employed in tying Chrysanthemum blooms to little sticks.

" I'm bothered about a cook," she said.

" And I, about a maid ! I dismissed ffoliott this morning—well I simply *had* to —for a figure salient."

" So awkward out here to replace any-one ; I'm sure I don't know . . ." the Ambassadress replied, her eyes hovering tragically over the pantaloons strained to *splitting* point, of the stooping gardener.

"It's a pretty prospect. . . ."

"Life is a compound!" Lady Something defined it at last.

Mrs Chilleywater turned surprised. "Not even Socrates," she declared, "said anything truer than that."

"A compound!" Lady Something twittered again.

"I should like to put that into the lips of Delitsiosa."

"Who's Delitsiosa?" the Ambassadress asked as a smothered laugh broke out beside her.

Mrs Chilleywater looked up.

"I'd forgotten you were there. Strange thing among the cedar-boughs," she said.

The Hon. Lionel Limpness tossed a slippered foot flexibly from his hammock.

"You may well ask 'who's Delitsiosa'!" he exclaimed.

"She is my new heroine," Mrs Chilleywater replied, after a few quick little clutches at her hair.

"I trust you won't treat her, dear, quite so shamefully as your last."

The Authoress tittered.

" Delitsiosa is the wife of Marsden Did-
cote," she said, " the manager of a pawn-
shop in the district of Maida Vale, and in
the novel he seduces an innocent seamstress,
Iris Drummond, who comes in one day to
redeem her petticoat (and really I don't
know how I did succeed in drawing the
portrait of a little fool !) . . . and when
Delitsiosa, her suspicions aroused, can no
longer doubt or ignore her husband's intimacy with Iris, already engaged to a lusty
young farmer in Kent—(some boy)—she
decides to yield herself to the entreaties of
her brother-in-law Percy, a junior partner
in the firm, which brings about the great
tussle between the two brothers on the
edge of the Kentish cliffs. Iris and Delitsiosa—Iris is anticipating a babelet soon—
are watching them from a cornfield, where
they're boiling a kettle for afternoon tea ;
and oh, I've such a darling description of a
cornfield. I make you *feel* England ! "

" No really, my dear," Lady Something
exclaimed.

" Harold pretends it would be wonderful,
arranged as an Opera . . . with duos and

things and a *Liebestod* for Delitzi towards the close."

"No, no," Mr Limpness protested : "What would become of our modern fiction at all if Victoria Gellybore Frinton gave herself up to the stage ? "

"That's quite true, strange thing among the cedar-boughs," Mrs Chilleywater returned fingering the floating strings of the bandelette at her brow : "It's lamentable ; yet who is there doing anything at present for English Letters . . . ? Who among us to-day," she went on peering up at him, "is carrying on the tradition of Fielding ? Who really cares ? I know *I* do what I can . . . and there's Madam Adrian Bloater, of course. But I can think of no one else ;—we two."

Mr Limpness rocked, critically.

"I can't bear Bloater's books," he demurred.

"To be frank, neither can I. I'm very fond of Lilian Bloater, I adore her *weltbürgerliche* nature, but I feel like you about her books ; I *cannot* read them. If only she would forget Adrian ; but she will thrust him headlong into all her work.

THE FLOWER BENEATH THE FOOT

Have *I* ever drawn Harold? No. (Although many of the public seem to think so!) And please heaven, however *great* my provocation at times may be, I never shall!"

"And there I think you're right," the Ambassadress answered, frowning a little as the refrain that her daughter was singing caught her ear.

> "And when I sees 'im
> My heart goes BOOM! . . .
> And I topple over ;
> I topple over, over, over,
> All for Love!"

"I dreamt last night my child was on the Halls."

"There's no doubt, she'd dearly like to be."

"Her Father would never hear of it!"

> "And when she sees me
> O, when she sees me—
> (*The voice slightly false was Harold's*)
> Her heart goes BOOM! . . .
> And she topples over ;
> She topples over, over, over,
> All for Love!"

"There ; they've routed Sir Some-body. . . ."

"And when anything vexes him," Lady Something murmured, appraising the Ambassador's approaching form with a glassy eye, "he always, you know, blames me ! "

Shorn of the sombre, betailed attire, so indispensable for the town-duties of a functionary, Sir Somebody, while rusticating, usually wore a white-twill jacket, and black multi-pleated pantaloons ; while for headgear, he would favour a Mexican sugar-loaf, or green-draped pugaree : "He looks half-Irish," Lady Something would sometimes say.

"Infernal Bedlam," he broke out : "the house is sheer pandemonium."

"I found it so too, dear," Lady Something agreed ; "and so," she added, removing a fallen tree-bug tranquilly from her hair, "I've been digesting my letters out here upon the lawn."

"And no doubt," Sir Somebody murmured, fixing the placid person of his wife, with a keen psychological glance : "you succeed, my dear, in digesting them ? "

" Why shouldn't I ? "

" . . . " the Ambassador displayed discretion.

" We're asked to a Lion hunt in the Land of Dates; quite an *entreating* invitation from the dear Queen—; really most pressing and affectionate, but Princess Elsie's nuptial negotiations and this pending Procès with the Ritz, may tie us here for some time."

" Ah Rosa."

" Why these constant moans ? . . .? A clairvoyant once told me I'd 'the bump of Litigation '—a *cause célèbre* unmistakably defined ; so it's as well, on the whole, to have it over."

" And quite probably ; had your statement been correct——"

The Ambassadress gently glowed.

" I'm told it's simply swarming ! " she impenitently said.

" Oh Rosa, Rosa. . . ."

" And if you doubt it at all, here is an account direct from the Ritz itself," her Excellency replied, singling out a letter from among the rest : " It is from dear old

General Sir Trotter-Stormer. He says :
' I am the only guest here. I must say,
however, the attendance is beyond all
praise, more *soigné* and better than I've
ever known it to be, but after what you
told me, dear friend, I feel *distinctly uncom-
fortable* when the hour for bye-bye comes ! ' "

" Pish ; what evidence, pray, is that ? "

" I regard it as of the very first importance ! Sir Trotter admits—a distinguished
soldier admits, his uneasiness ; and who
knows, he is so brave about concealing his
woes—his two wives left him !—what he may
not have patiently and stoically endured ? "

" Less I am sure, my dear, than I of late
in listening sometimes to you. "

" I will write I think and press him for a
more detailed report. . . ."

The Ambassador turned away.

" She should no more be trusted with ink
than a child with firearms ! " he declared,
addressing himself with studious indirect-
ness to a garden-snail.

Lady Something blinked.

" Life is a compound," she murmured
again.

THE FLOWER BENEATH THE FOOT

" Particularly for women ! " the Authoress agreed.

" Ah, well," the Ambassadress majestic-
ally rose : " I must be off and issue house-
hold orders ; although I derive hardly my
usual amount of enjoyment at present, I
regret to say, from my morning consulta-
tions with the cook. . . ."

XI

IT had been once the whim, and was
now the felicitous habit of the Countess
of Tolga to present Count Cabinet
annually with a bouquet of flowers. It was
as if Venus-Anadyomene herself, standing [1]
on a shell and wafted by all the piquant
whispers of the town and court, would intrude upon the flattered exile (with her
well-wired orchids, and malicious, soulless,
laughter), to awaken delicate, pagan images,
of a trecento, Tuscan Greece.

But upon this occasion desirous of intro-
ducing some new features, the Countess
decided on presenting the fallen senator
with a pannier of well-grown, early pears,
a small "heath," and the Erotic Poems
bound in half calf with tasteful tooling of a
Schoolboy Poet, cherishable chiefly, perhaps, for the vignette frontispiece of the
author. Moreover, acting on an impulse

[1] *Vide* Botticelli.

155

she was never able afterwards to explain, she had invited Mademoiselle Olga Blumenghast to accompany her.

Never had summer shown a day more propitiously clement, than the afternoon in mid-Autumn they prepared to set out.

Fond of a compliment, when not too frankly racy,[1] and knowing how susceptible the exile was to clothes, the Countess had arrayed herself in a winter gown of kingfisher-tinted silk turning to turquoise, and stencilled in purple at the arms and neck with a crisp Greek-key design ; while a voluminous violet veil, depending behind her to a point, half-concealed a tricorne turquoise toque from which arose a shaded lilac aigrette branching several ways.

" I shall probably die with heat, and of course it's most unsuitable ; but poor old man, he likes to recall the Capital ! " the Countess panted, as, nursing heath, poems and pears, she followed Mademoiselle Olga Blumenghast blindly towards the shore.

Oars, and swaying drying nets, a skyline

[1] In Pisuerga compliments are apt to rival in this respect those of the ardent South.

lost in sun, a few moored craft beneath the little rickety wooden pier awaiting choice : —" The boatmen, to-day, darling, seem all so ugly ; let's take a sailing-boat and go alone ! "

" I suppose there's no danger, darling ? " the Countess replied, and scarcely had she time to make any slight objection, than the owner of a steady wide-bottomed boat—the *Calypso*—was helping them to embark.

The Island of St Helena, situated towards the lake's bourne, lay distant some two miles or more, and within a short way of the open sea.

With sails distended to a languid breeze the shore eventually was left behind ; and the demoiselle cranes, in mid-lake, were able to observe there were two court dames among them.

" Although he's dark, Vi," Mademoiselle Olga Blumenghast presently exclaimed, dropping her cheek to a frail hand upon the tiller, " although he's dark, it's odd how he gives one the impression somehow of perfect fairness ! "

"Who's that, darling ? " the Countess

murmured, appraising with fine eyes, faintly weary, the orchid-like style of beauty of her friend.

" Ann-Jules, of course."

" I begin to wish, do you know, I'd brought Pomegranates, and worn something else ! "

"What are those big burley-worleys ? "

" Pears. . . ."

" Give me one."

" Catch, then."

" Not that I could bear to be married ; especially like *you*, Vi ! "

" A marriage like ours, dear, was so utterly unworthwhile. . . ."

" I'm not sure, dear, that I comprehend altogether ? "

" Seagulls' wings as they fan one's face. . . ."

" It's vile and wrong to shoot them : but oh ! How I wish your happiness depended, even ever so little, on me."

The Countess averted her eyes

Waterfowl, like sadness passing, hovered, and soared overhead, casting their dark, fleeting shadows to the white, drowned clouds, in the receptive waters of the lake.

" I begin to wish I'd brought grapes," she breathed.

"Heavy stodgy pears. So do I."

" Or a few special peaches," the Countess murmured, taking up the volume of verse beside her, with a little, mirthless, half-hysterical laugh.

To a Faithless Friend.

To V.O.I. and S.C.P.

For Stephen.

When the Dormitory Lamp burns Low.

Her gaze travelled over the Index.

" Read something, dear," Mademoiselle Blumenghast begged, toying with the red-shaded flower in her burnished curls.

" Gladly ; but oh, Olga ! " the Countess crooned.

"What ! "

"Where's the wind ? "

It had gone.

"We must row."

There was nothing for it.

To gain the long, white breakwater, with the immemorial willow-tree at its end, that was the most salient feature of the island's approach, required, nevertheless, resolution.

" It's so far, dear," the Countess kept on saying. " I had no idea how far it was ! Had you any conception at all it was so far ? "

" Let us await the wind, then. It's bound to rally."

But no air swelled the sun-bleached sails, or disturbed the pearly patine of the paralysed waters.

" I shall never get this peace, I only realise it *exists* . . ." the Countess murmured with dream-glazed eyes.

" It's astonishing . . . the stillness," Mademoiselle Blumenghast murmured, with a faint tremor, peering round towards the shore.

On the banks young censia-trees raised their boughs like strong white whips towards the mountains, upon whose loftier heights lay, here and there, a little stray patch of snow.

" Come hither, ye winds, come hither ! " she softly called.

" Oh, Olga ! Do we really want it ? " the Countess in agitation asked, discarding her hat and veil with a long, sighing breath.

"I don't know, dear; no; not, not much."

"Nor I,—at all."

"Let us be patient then."

"It's all so beautiful it makes one want to cry."

"Yes; it makes one want to cry," Mademoiselle Blumenghast murmured, with a laugh that in brilliance vied with the October sun.

"Olga!"

"So," as the *Calypso* lurched: "lend me your hanky, dearest."

"*Olga*—?—? Thou fragile, and exquisite thing!"

.   .   .   .

Meanwhile Count Cabinet was seated with rod-and-line at an open window, idly ogling a swan. Owing to the reluctance of tradespeople to call for orders, the banished statesman was often obliged to supplement the larder himself. But hardly had he been angling ten minutes to-day, when lo! a distinguished mauvish fish with vivid scarlet spots. Pondering on the mysteries of the deep, and of the subtle variety there

is in Nature, the veteran ex-minister lit a
cigar. Among the more orthodox types
that stocked the lake, such as carp, cod,
tench, eels, sprats, shrimps, etc., this ex-
ceptional fish must have known its trials
and persecutions, its hours of superior
difficulty . . . and the Count, with a stoic
smile recalled his own. Musing on the
advantages and disadvantages of person-
ality, of " party " viewpoints, and of
morals in general, the Count was soon too
self-absorbed to observe the approach of
his " useful " secretary and amanuensis,
Peter Passer.

More valet perhaps than secretary, and
more errand-boy than either, the former
chorister of the Blue Jesus had followed
the fallen statesman into exile at a moment
when the Authorities of Pisuerga were
making minute enquiries for sundry
missing articles,[1] from the *Trésor* of the

---

[1] The missing articles were :—
    5 chasubles.
    A relic-casket in lapis and diamonds, containing the
      Tongue of St Thelma.
    4¾ yards of black lace, said to have " belonged " to the
      Madonna.

Cathedral, and since the strain of constant choir-practice is apt to be injurious for a youngster suffering from a delicate chest, the adolescent had been willing enough to accept, for a time, at least, a situation in the country.

" O, sir," he exclaimed, and almost in his excitement forgetting altogether the insidious, lisping tones he preferred as a rule to employ : " O, sir, here comes that old piece of rubbish again with a fresh pack of tracts ! "

" Collect yourself, Peter, pray do : what, lose our heads for a visit ? " the Count said getting up and going to a glass.

" I've noticed, sir, it's impossible to live on an island long without feeling its effects ; you *can't* escape being insular ! "

" Or insolent."

" Insular, sir ! "

" No matter much, but if it's the Countess Yvorra, you might shew her round the garden this time, perhaps, for a change," the Count replied, adjusting a demure-looking fly, of indeterminate sex, to his line.

And brooding on life and baits, and what *A* will come for while *B* won't, the Count's thoughts grew almost humorous as the afternoon wore on.

Evening was approaching, when weary of the airs of a common carp, he drew in, at length, his tackle.

Like a shawl of turquoise silk the lake seemed to vie, in serenity and radiance, with the bluest day in June, and it was no surprise, on descending presently for a restricted ramble—(the island, in all, amounted to scarcely one acre)—to descry the invaluable Peter enjoying a pleasant swim.

When not boating or reading or feeding his swans, to watch Peter's fancy-diving off the terrace end, was perhaps the favourite pastime of the veteran *viveur*: to behold the lad trip along the riven breakwater, as naked as a statue, shoot out his arms and spring, the *Flying-head-leap* or the *Backsadilla*, was a beautiful sight, looking up now and again—but more often *now*—from a volume of old Greek verse ; while to hear him warbling in the water with his clear alto voice—of Kyries and Anthems he knew no end—would often stir the old man to the point of tears. Frequently the swans themselves would paddle up to listen, expressing by the charmed or rapturous motions of their necks (recalling to the exile the ecstasies of certain musical, or "artistic" dames at Concert-halls, or the Opera House, long ago) their mute appreciation, their touched delight. . . .

"Old goody Two-shoes never came, sir," Peter archly lisped, admiring his adventurous shadow upon the breakwater wall.

"How is that?"

"Becalmed, sir," Peter answered, culling languidly a small, nodding rose, that was clinging to the wall:

"O becalmed is my soul
I rejoice in the Lord!"

At one extremity of the garden stood the Observatory, and after duly appraising various of Peter's neatest feats, the Count strolled away towards it. But before he could reach the Observatory, he had first to pass his swans.

They lived, with an ancient water-wheel, beneath a cupola of sun-glazed tiles, sheltered, partially, from the lake by a hedge of towering red geraniums, and the Count seldom wearied of watching these strangely gorgeous creatures as they sailed out and in through the sanguine-hued flowers. A few, with their heads sunk back beneath their wings, had retired for the night already ; nevertheless, the Count paused to shake a finger at one somnolent bird, in disfavour for pecking Peter : " Jealous, doubtless of the lad's grace," he mused, fumbling with the key of the Observatory door.

The unrivalled instrument that the Observatory contained, whose intricate lenses were capable of drawing even the remote Summer-Palace to within an appreciable range, was, like most instruments of merit, sensitive to the manner of its manipulation ; and fearing lest the inexpert tampering of a homesick housekeeper (her native village was visible in clear weather, with the aid of a glass) should break or injure the delicate lenses, the

Count kept the Observatory usually under key.

But the inclination to focus the mundane, and embittered features of the fanatic Countess, as she lectured her boatmen for forgetting their oars, or, being considerably superstitious, to count the moles on their united faces as an esoteric clue to the Autumn Lottery, waned a little before the mystery of the descending night.

Beneath a changing tide of deepening shadow, the lifeless valleys were mirroring to the lake the sombreness of dusk. Across the blue forlornness of the water, a swan, here and there, appeared quite violet, while coiffed in swift clinging, golden clouds, the loftiest hills alone retained the sun.

A faint nocturnal breeze, arising simultaneously with the Angelus-bell, seemed likely to relieve, at the moon's advent, the trials to her patience of the Countess Yvorra: "who must be cursing," the Count reflected, turning the telescope about with a sigh, to suit her sail.

Ah poignant moments when the heart

stops still ! Not since the hour of his exile
had the Count's been so arrested.

From the garden Peter's voice rose
questingly ; but the Count was too wonder-
struck, far, to heed it.

Caught in the scarlet radiance of the
afterglow, the becalmed boat, for one brief
and most memorable second, was his to
gaze on.

In certain lands with what diplomacy
falls the night, and how discreetly is the
daylight gone : Those dimmer-and-dimmer,
darker-and-lighter twilights of the North,
so disconcerting in their playfulness, were
unknown altogether in Pisuerga. There,
Night pursued Day, as though she meant
it. No lingering, or arctic sentiment ! No
concertinaishness. . . . Hard on the sun's
heels, pressed Night. And the wherefore of
her haste ; Sun-attraction ? Impatience to
inherit ? An answer to such riddles as these
may doubtless be found by turning to the
scientists' theories on Time and Relativity.

Effaced in the blue air of evening became
everything, and with the darkness returned
the wind.

"Sir, sir? . . . Ho, Hi, hiiiiiiiiiiii!!" Peter's voice came again.

But transfixed, and loath just then for company, the Count made no reply.

A green-lanterned barge passed slowly, coming from the sea, and on the mountain-side a village light winked wanly here and there.

"Oh, why was I not *sooner*?" he murmured distractedly aloud.

.   .   .   .

"Oh Olga!"

"Oh Vi!"

" . . . I hope you've enough money for the boat, dear? . . .?"

" . . .!!?"

"Tell me, Olga: Is my hat all side-ways?"

" . . . ."

The long windows of the Summer-Palace were staring white to the moon, as the Countess of Tolga, her aigrettes casting *heroic* shadows and hugging still her heath, re-entered the Court's precincts on the arm of her friend.

XII

ONE evening, as Mrs Montgomery was reading *Vanity Fair* for the fifteenth time, there came a tap at the door. It was not the first interruption since opening the cherished green-bound book, and Mrs Montgomery seemed disinclined to stir. With the Court about to return to winter quarters, and the Summer-Palace upside down, the royal governess was still able to command her habitual British phlegm. It had been decided, moreover, that she should remain behind in the forsaken palace with the little prince, the better to "prepare" him for his forthcoming Eton exam.

Still, with disputes as to the precedence of trunks and dress-baskets simmering in the corridors without, it was easier to enjoy the Barley-sugar stick in one's mouth, than the Novel in one's hand.

"Thank God I'm not touchy!" Mrs

Montgomery reflected, rolling her eyes lazily about the little white wainscoted room.

It was as if something of her native land had crept in through the doorway with her, so successfully had she inculcated its tendencies, or spiritual Ideals, upon everything around.

A solitary teapot, on a bracket, above the door, two *Jubilee* plates, some peacocks' feathers, an image of a little Fisher-boy in bathing-drawers and a broken hand ;—" a work of delicate beauty ! " A mezzotint : *The Coiffing of Maria*—these were some of the treasures which the room contained.

" A blessing to be sure when the Court has gone ! " she reflected half-rising to drop a curtsy to Prince Olaf who had entered.

" Word from your country," sententiously he broke out : " My brother's betrothed ! So need I go on with my preparation ? "

" Put your tie straight ! And just look at your socks all tumbling down. Such great jambons of knees ! . . . What will become of you, I ask myself, when you're a lower boy at Eton."

" How can I be a lower boy when I'm a Prince ? "

" Probably, the Rev. Ruggles-White, when you enter his House, will be able to explain. "

" I won't be a lower boy ! I will *not* ! "

" Cs, Cs. "

" Damn the democracy. "

" Fie, sir. "

" Down with it. "

" For shame. "

" Revenge. "

" That will do : and now, let me hear your lessons : I should like," Mrs Montgomery murmured, her eyes set in detachment upon the floor ; " the present-indicative tense of the Verb *To be* ! Adding the words, Political h-Hostess ;—more for the sake of the pronunciation than for anything else. "

And after considerable persuasion, prompting, and " bribing," with various sorts of sweets :

" I am a Political Hostess,
  Thou art a Political Hostess,

He is a Political Hostess,
We are Political Hostesses,
Ye are Political Hostesses,
They are Political Hostesses."

"Very good, dear, and only one mistake. *He* is a Political h-Hostess: Can
you correct yourself? The error is so
slight. . . . . ."

But alas the prince was in no mood for
study; and Mrs Montgomery very soon
afterwards was obliged to let him go.

Moving a little anxiously about the
room, her meditations turned upon the
future.

With the advent of Elsie a new régime
would be established: increasing Britishers
would wish to visit Pisuerga; and it
seemed a propitious moment to abandon
teaching, and to inaugurate in Kairoulla an
English hotel.

"I have no more rooms. I am quite
full up!" she smiled, addressing the silver
andirons in the grate.

And what a deliverance to have done
with instructing unruly children, she

reflected, going towards the glass mail-box attached to her vestibule door. Sometimes about this hour there would be a letter in it, but this evening there was only a picture postcard of a field mouse in a bonnet, from her old friend Mrs Bedley.

"We have *Valmouth* at last," she read, "and was it you, my dear, who asked for *The Beard Throughout the Ages*? It is in much demand, but I am keeping it back anticipating a *reply*. Several of the plates are missing I see, among them, those of the late King Edward, and of Assur Bani Pal; I only mention it, that, you may know I shan't blame you! We are having wonderful weather, and I am keeping pretty well, although poor Mrs Barleymoon, I fear, will not see through another winter. Trusting you are benefiting by the beautiful country air : your obedient servant to command, ANN BEDLEY.

"P.S.—*Man, and All About Him*, is rebinding. Ready I expect soon."

"Ah! Cunnie, Cunnie . . . ?" Mrs Montgomery murmured, laying the card down near a photograph of the Court-physician with a sigh : " Ah ! Arthur Amos Cuncliffe Babcock . . . ? " she invoked his name dulcetly in full : and as though in telepathic response, there came a tap at the door, and the doctor himself looked in.

He had been attending, it seemed, the young wife of the Comptroller of the House-hold at the extremity of the corridor ; a creature, who, after two brief weeks of marriage, imagined herself to be in an interesting state : " *I believe baby's com-ing* ! " she would cry out every few hours.

" Do I intrude ? " he demanded, in his forceful, virile voice, that ladies knew and liked : " pray say so if I do."

" Does he intrude ! " Mrs Montgomery flashed an arch glance towards the cornice.

" Well, and how are you keeping ? " the doctor asked, dropping on to a rep causeuse that stood before the fire.

" I'm only semi-well, doctor, thanks ! "

" Why, what's the trouble ? "

" You know my organism is not a very strong one, Dr Cuncliffe . . ." Mrs Mont-gomery replied, drawing up a chair, and

175

settling a cushion with a sigh of resignation at her back.

" Imagination ! "

" If only it were ! "

" Imagination," he repeated, fixing a steady eye on the short train of her black brocaded robe that all but brushed his feet.

" If that's your explanation for continuous broken sleep . . ." she gently snapped.

" Try mescal. "

" I'm trying Dr Fritz Millar's treatment," the lady stated, desiring to deal a slight *scratch* to his masculine *amour propre*.

" Millar's an Ass. "

" I don't agree at all ! " she incisively returned, smiling covertly at his touch of pique.

" What is it ? "

" Oh it's horrid. You first of all lie down ; and then you drink cold water in the sun."

" Cold what ? I never *heard* of such a thing : It's enough to kill you."

Mrs Montgomery took a deep-drawn breath of languor.

THE FLOWER BENEATH THE FOOT

" And would you care, doctor, so *very* much if it did ? " she asked, as a page made his appearance with an ice-bucket and champagne.

" To toast our young Princess ! "

" Oh, oh, Dr Cuncliffe ? What a wicked man you are : " And for a solemn moment their thoughts went out in unison to the sea-girt land of their birth — Barkers', Selfridges', Brighton-pier, the Zoological gardens on a Sunday afternoon.

" Here's to the good old country ! " the doctor quaffed.

" The Bride, and," Mrs Montgomery raised her glass, " the Old Folks at h-home."

" The Old Folks at home ! " he vaguely echoed.

" Bollinger, you naughty man," the lady murmured, amiably seating herself on the causeuse at his side.

" You'll find it dull here all alone after the Court has gone," he observed, smiling down, a little despotically, on to her bright, abundant hair.

Mrs Montgomery sipped her wine.

" When the wind goes whistling up and

down under the colonnades : oh, then ! "
she shivered.

" You'll wish for a fine, bold Pisuergian
husband ; shan't you ? " he answered, his
foot drawing closer to hers.

" Often of an evening, I feel I need
fostering," she owned, glancing up yearn-
ingly into his face.

" Fostering, eh ? " he chuckled, refilling
with exuberance her glass.

" Why is it that wine always makes me
feel *so good* ? "

" Probably, because it fills you with
affection for your neighbour ! "

" It's true ; I feel I could be very affectionate : I'm what they call an 'amoureuse'
I suppose, and there it is. . . ."

There fell a busy silence between them.

" It's almost too warm for a fire," she
murmured, repairing towards the window ;
" but I like to hear the crackle ! "

" Company, eh ? " he returned, following
her (a trifle unsteadily) across the room.

" The night is so clear the moon looks to
be almost transparent," she languorously
observed, with a long tugging sigh.

" And so it does," he absently agreed.

" I adore the Pigeons in my wee court towards night, when they sink down like living sapphires upon the stones," she sentimentally said, sighing languorously again.

" Ours," he assured her ; " since the surgery looks on to it, too. . . ."

" Did you ever see anything so ducky-wucky, so completely twee ! " she inconsequently chirruped.

" Allow me to fill this empty glass."

" I want to go out on all that gold floating water ! " she murmured listlessly, pointing towards the lake.

" Alone ? "

" Drive me towards the sweet seaside," she begged, taking appealingly his hand.

" Aggie ? "

" Arthur—Arthur, for God's sake ! " she shrilled, as with something between a snarl and a roar, he impulsively whipped out the light.

" H-Help ! Oh Arth——"

Thus did they celebrate the " Royal engagement."

XIII

BEHIND the heavy moucharabi in the little dark shop of Haboubet of Egypt all was song, *fête* and preparation. Additional work, had brought additional hands, and be-tarbouched boys in burnooses, and baskets of blossoms, lay strewn all over the floor.

" Sweet is the musk-rose of the Land of Punt !
Sweet are the dates from Khorassân . . .
But bring *me* (O wandering Djinns) the English rose, the English apple !
O sweet is the land of the Princess Elsie,
Sweet indeed is England——"

Bachir's voice soared, in improvisation, to a long-drawn, strident, wail.

" Pass me the scissors, O Bachir ben Ahmed, for the love of Allah," a young man with large lucent eyes, and an untroubled

face, like a flower, exclaimed, extending a
slender, keef-stained hand.

"Sidi took them," the superintendent
of the Duchess of Varna replied, turning
towards an olive-skinned Armenian youth,
who, seated on an empty hamper, was
reading to a small, rapt group, the
Kairoulla Intelligence aloud.

" 'Attended by Lady Canon-of-Noon
and by Lady Bertha Chamberlayne (she is
a daughter of Lord Frollo's [1]) the Princess
was seen to alight from her saloon, in a
chic toque of primrose paille, stabbed
with the quill of a nasturtium-coloured
bird, and, darting forward, like the Bird
of Paradise that she *is*, embraced her
future Parents-in-law with considerable
affection. . . .' "

" Scissors, for the love of Allah ! "

" ' And soon I heard the roll of drums !
And saw the bobbing plumes in the jangling
browbands of the horses : it was a moment
I shall never forget. She passed . . . and

[1] Although the account of Princess Elsie's arrival in
Kairoulla is signed "Green Jersey," it seems not unlikely
that "Eva Schnerb" herself was the reporter on this
eventful occasion.

as our Future Sovereign turned smiling to bow her acknowledgments to the crowd, I saw a happy tear . . . ! ' "

" Ah Allah."

" Pass me two purple pinks."

" ' Visibly gratified at the cordial ovation to her Virgin Daughter was Queen Glory, a striking and impressive figure, all a-glitter in a splendid dark dress of nacre and nigger tissue, her many Orders of Merit almost bearing her down.' "

" Thy scissors, O Sidi, for the love of Muhammed ? "

" ' It seemed as if Kairoulla had gone wild with joy. Led by the first Life-Guards and a corps of ladies of great fashion disguised as peasants, the cortège proceeded amid the whole-hearted plaudits of the people towards Constitutional Square, where, with the sweetest of smiles and thanks the princess received an exquisite sheaf of Deflas (they are the hybrids of slipper-orchids crossed with maidens-rue, and are all the mode at present), tendered her by little Paula Exelmans, the Lord Mayor's tiny daughter. Driving on, amid showers

of confetti, the procession passed up the
Chausée, which presented a scene of rare
animation ; boys, and even quite elderly
dames swarming up the trees to obtain a
better view of their new Princess. But it
was not until Lilianthal Street and the
Cathedral Square were reached, that the
climax reached its height ! Here, a short
standstill was called, and after an appro-
priate address from the Archbishop of
Pisuerga, the stirring strains of the National
Anthem, superbly rendered by Madame
Marguerite Astorra of the State Theatre
(she is in perfect voice this season), arose
on the air. At that moment a black cat
and its kitties rushed across the road, and
I saw the Princess smile.' "

" Thy scissors, O Sidi, in the Name of
the Prophet ! "

" ' A touching incident,' " Sidi with
equanimity pursued, " ' was just before the
English Tea Rooms, where the English
Colony had mustered together in force. . . .' "

But alack for those interested. Owing
to the clamour about him much of the
recital was lost : " ' Cheers and tears. . . .

. . . Life's benison. . . . Honiton lace. . . .
If I live to be *forty*, it was a moment I shall
never forget. . . . Panic . . . congestion.
. . . Police.' "

But it was scarcely needful to peruse
the paper, when on the boulevards outside, the festivities were everywhere in full
swing. The arrival of the princess for her
wedding had brought to Kairoulla unpre-
cedented crowds from all parts of the
kingdom, as much eager to see the princess,
as to catch a glimpse of the fine pack of
beagles, that it was said had been brought
over with her, and which had taken an
half eerie hold of the public mind.
Gilderoy, Beausire, Audrey, many of the
dogs' names were known pleasantly to the
crowd already ; and anecdotes of Audrey,
picture-postcards of Audrey, were sold as
rapidly almost as those even of the princess.
Indeed mothers among the people had
begun to threaten their disobedient offspring with Audrey, whose silky, thickset
frame was supported, it appeared, daily on
troublesome little boys and tiresome little
girls. . . .

" Erri, erri, get on with thy bouquet, oh Lazari Demitraki ! " Bachir exclaimed in plaintive tones, addressing a blonde boy with a skin of amber, who was " charming " an earwig with a reed of grass.

" She dance the *Boussadilla* just like in the street of Halfaouine in Gardaïa my town any Ouled Naïl ! " he rapturously gurgled.

" Get on with thy work, oh Lazari Demitraki," Bachir besought him, " and leave the earwigs alone for the clients to find."

" What with the heat, the smell of the flowers, the noise of you boys, and with filthy earwigs Boussadillaing all over one, I feel I could *swoon*," the voice, cracked yet cloying, was Peter Passer's.

He had come to Kairoulla for the " celebrations," and also, perhaps, aspiring to advance his fortunes, in ways known best to himself. With Bachir, his connection dated from long ago, when as a Cathedral choir-boy it had been his habit to pin a shoulder, or bosom-blossom to his surplice, destroying it with coquettish, ring-laden fingers in the course of an anthem, and scattering the petals from the choir-loft, leaf by leaf, on to the grey heads of the monsignori below.

" Itchiata wa ? " Bachir grumbled, playing his eyes distractedly around the shop. And it might have been better for the numerous orders there were to attend to had he called fewer of his acquaintance to assist him. Sunk in torpor, a cigarette smouldering at his ear, a Levantine Greek known as " Effendi darling " was listening to a dark-cheeked Tunisian engaged at the Count of Tolga's private Hammam Baths— a young man, who, as he spoke, would make mazy gestures of the hands as though his master's ribs, or those of some illustrious guest, lay under him. But by no means all of those assembled in the little shop, bore the seal of Islam. An American who had grown too splendid for the copper " Ganymede " or Soda-fountain of a Café bar and had taken to teaching the hectic dance-steps of his native land in the night-halls where Bachir sold, was achieving wonders with some wires and Eucharist

THE FLOWER BENEATH THE FOOT

lilies, while discussing with a shy-mannered
youth the many difficulties that beset the
foreigner in Kairoulla.

"Young chaps that come out here,
don't know what they're coming to," he
sapiently remarked, using his incomparable
teeth in place of scissors. "Gosh! Talk
of advancement," he growled.

"There's few can mix as I can, yet I
don't never get no rise!" the shy youth
exclaimed, producing a card that was
engraved: *Harry Cummings, Salad-Dresser
to the King:* "I expect I've arrived," he
murmured, turning to hide a modest blush
towards a pale young man who looked on
life through heavy horn glasses.

"Salad dressing? I'd sooner it was hair!
You do get tips there anyway," the Yankee
reasoned.

"I wish *I* were—arrived," the young
man with the glasses, by name Guy Thin,
declared. He had come out but recently
from England to establish a "British
Grocery," and was the owner of what is
sometimes called an expensive voice, his
sedulously clear articulation missing out

187

no syllable or letter of anything he might happen to be saying, as though he were tasting each word, like the Pure tea, or the Pure marmalade, or any other of the so very Pure goods he proposed so exclusively to sell.

"If Allah wish it then you arrive," Lazari Demitraki assured him with a dazzling smile, catching his hand in order to construe the lines.

"Finish thy bouquet, O Lazari Demitraki," Bachir faintly moaned.

"It finished—arranged : it with Abou ! " he announced, pointing to an aged negro with haunted sin-sick eyes who appeared to be making strange grimaces at the wall. A straw hat of splendid dimensions was on his head, flaunting bravely the insignia of the Firm.

But the old man seemed resolved to run no more errands :

"Nsa, nsa," he mumbled : " Me walk enough for one day ! Me no go out any more. Old Abou too tired to take another single step ! As soon would me cross the street again dis night as the Sahara ! . . ."

And it was only after the promise of a small gift of Opium that he consented to leave a débutante's bouquet at the Théâtre Diana.[1]

"In future," Bachir rose remarking, "I only employ the women; I keep only girls," he repeated, for the benefit of "Effendi darling" who appeared to be attaining Nirvâna.

"And next I suppose you keep a Harem?" "Effendi darling" somnolently returned.

Most of the city shops had closed their shutters for the day, when Bachir shouldering a pannier bright with blooms, stepped with his companions forth into the street.

Along the Boulevards thousands were pressing towards the Regina Gardens to view the Fireworks, all agog to witness the pack of beagles wrought in brilliant lights due to course a stag across the sky, and which would change, if newspaper reports might be believed, at the critical moment,

---

[1] The Théâtre Diana; a Music Hall dedicated to Spanish Zarzuelas and Operettes. It enjoyed a somewhat doubtful reputation.

into " ' something of the nature of a surprise.' "

Pausing before a plate-glass window that adjoined the shop to adjust the flowing folds of his gandourah, and to hoist his flower tray to his small scornful head, Bachir allowed his auxiliaries to drift, mostly two by two, away among the crowd. Only the royal salad-dresser, Harry Cummings, expressed a demure inclination (when the pushing young grocer caressed his arm), to " be alone " ; but Guy Thin, who had private designs upon him, was loath to hear of it ! He wished to persuade him to buy a bottle of Vinegar from his Store, when he would print on his paper-bags *As supplied to his Majesty the King*.

" Grant us, O Allah, each good Fortunes," Bachir beseeched, looking up through his eyelashes towards the moon, that drooped like a silver amulet in the firmament above : in the blue nocturnal air he looked like a purple poppy. " A toute à l'heure mes amis ! " he murmured as he moved away.

And in the little closed shop behind the heavy moucharabi, now that they all had gone, the exhalations of the *flowers* arose ; pungent, concerted odours, expressive of natural antipathies and feuds, suave alliances, suffering, pride, and joy. . . . Only the shining moon through the moucharabi, illumining here a lily, there a leaf, may have guessed what they were saying :

"My wires are hurting me : my wires are hurting me."

"I have no water. I cannot reach the water."

"They have pushed me head down into the bottom of the bowl."

"I'm glad I'm in a Basket ! No one will hurl *me* from a window to be bruised under foot by the callous crowd."

"It's uncomfy, isn't it, without one's roots ? "

"You Weed you ! You, you, you . . . *buttercup* ! How dare you to *an Orchid* ! "

"I shouldn't object to sharing the same water with him, dear . . . Ordinary as he is ! If *only* he wouldn't smell. . . ."

"She's nothing but a piece of common grass and so I tell her ! "

THE FLOWER BENEATH THE FOOT

When upon the tense pent atmosphere surged a breath of cooler air, and through the street-door slipped the Duchess of Varna.

Overturning a jar of great heavy-headed Gladioli with a crash, she sailed, with a purposeful step, towards the till.

Garbed in black and sleepy citrons, she seemed, indeed, to be equipped for a long, long Voyage, and was clutching, in her arms, a pet Poodle dog, and a levant-covered case, in which, doubtless, reposed her jewels.

Since her rupture with Madame Wetme (both the King and Queen had refused to receive her), the money *ennuis* of the Duchess had become increasingly acute. Tormented by tradespeople, dunned and bullied by creditors, menaced, mortified, insulted—an offer to " star " in the *rôle* of *A Society Thief* for the cinematograph had particularly shocked her—the inevitable hour to quit the Court so long foreseen had come. And now with her departure definitely determined upon, the Duchess experienced an insouciance of heart unknown to her assuredly for many a year. Replenishing her reticule with quite a welcome sheaf of the elegant little bank-notes of Pisuerga, one thing only remained to do, and taking pen and paper, she addressed to the Editor of the *Intelligence* the supreme announcement :—" *The Duchess of Varna has left for Dateland.*"

Eight light words ! But enough to set *tout* Kairoulla in a rustle.

" I only so regret I didn't go sooner," she murmured to herself aloud, breaking herself a rose to match her gown from an arrangement in the window.

Many of the flowers had been newly christened, " Elsie," " Audrey," " London-Madonnas " (black Arums these), while the Roses from the " Land of Punt " had been renamed " Mrs Lloyd George "—and priced accordingly. A basket of Odonto-glossums eked out with Gypsophila seemed to anticipate the end, when supplies from Punt must necessarily cease. However, bright boys, like Bachir, seldom lacked patrons, and the duchess recalled glimpsing him one evening from her private sitting-room at the Ritz Hotel, seated on a garden bench in the Regina Gardens beside the

Prime Minister himself ; both, to all seem-
ing, on the most cordial terms, and to have
reached a perfect understanding as regards
the Eastern Question. Ah, the Eastern
Question! It was said that, in the Land of
Dates, one might study it well. In Djezira,
the chief town, beneath the great golden
sun, people, they said, might grow wise.
In the simoon that scatters the silver sand,
in the words of the nomads, in the fairy
mornings beneath the palms, society with
its foolish *cliché* . . . the duchess smiled.

"But for that poisonous woman, I should
have gone last year," she told herself,
interrupted in her cogitations by the
appearance of her maid.

"The train your Grace we shall miss
it. . . ."

"Nonsense!" the duchess answered
following, leaving the flowers alone again
to their subtle exhalations.

"I'm glad *I'm* in a Basket!"

"I have no water. I cannot reach the
water."

"Life's bound to be uncertain when you
haven't got your roots!"

XIV

ON a long-chair with tired, closed
eyes lay the Queen. Although
spared from henceforth the anxiety
of her son's morganatic marriage, yet, now
that his destiny was sealed, she could not
help feeling perhaps he might have done
better. The bride's lineage was nothing
to boast of—over her great-great-grand-
parents, indeed, in the year 17—it were
gentler to draw a veil—while, for the rest,
disingenuous, undistinguished, more at
home in the stables than in a drawing-
room, the Queen much feared that she and
her future daughter-in-law would scarcely
get on.

Yes, the little princess was none too
engaging, she reflected, and her poor
sacrificed child if not actually trapped . . .

The silken swish of a fan, breaking the
silence, induced the Queen to look up.

In waiting at present was the Countess

THE FLOWER BENEATH THE FOOT

Olivia d'Omptyda, a person of both excellent principles and birth, if lacking, somewhat, in social boldness. Whenever she entered the royal presence she would begin visibly to tremble, which considerably flattered the Queen. Her Father, Count "Freddie" d'Omptyda, an infantile and charming old man, appointed in a moment of unusual vagary Pisuergan Ambassador to the Court of St James', had lately married a child wife scarcely turned thirteen, whose frivolity, and numerous pranks on the high dames of London, were already the scandal of the *Corps Diplomatique*.

"Sssh! Noise is the last vulgarity," the Queen commented, raising a cushion embroidered with raging lions and white uncanny unicorns higher behind her head.

Unstrung from the numerous *fêtes*, she had retired to a distant boudoir to relax, and, having partly disrobed, was feeling remotely Venus of Miloey with her arms half-hidden in a plain white cape.

The Countess d'Omptyda furled her fan.

" In this Age of push and shriek . . ." she said and sighed.

THE FLOWER BENEATH THE FOOT

" It seems that neither King Geo, nor Queen Glory, *ever* lie down of a day ! " her Dreaminess declared.

" Since his last appointment, neither does Papa."

" The affair of your step-mother and Lady Diana Duff Semour," the Queen remarked, " appears to be assuming the proportions of an Incident ! "

The Countess dismally smiled. The subject of her step-mother, mistaken frequently for her grand-daughter, was a painful one : " I hear she's like a colt broke loose ! " she murmured, dropping her eyes fearfully to her costume.

She was wearing an apron of Parma-violets, and the Order of the Holy Ghost.

" It's a little a pity she can't be more sensible," the Queen returned, fingering listlessly some papers at her side. Among them was the *Archæological Society's* initial report relating to the recent finds among the Ruins of Sodom and Gomorrah. From Chedorlahomor came the good news that an *amphora* had been found, from which it seemed that men, in those days, rode sideways, and women straddle-legs, with their heads to the horses' tails, while a dainty cup, ravished from a rock-tomb in the Vale of Akko, ornamented with naked boys and goblets of flowers, encouraged a yet more extensive research.

" You may advance, Countess, with the Archæologists' report," the Queen commanded. " Omitting (skipping, I say) the death of the son of Lord Intriguer." [1]

" ' It was in the Vale of Akko, about two miles from Sââda," the Countess tremblingly began, " that we laid bare a superb tear-bottle, a unique specimen in *grisaille*, severely adorned with a matron's head. From the inscription, there can be no doubt whatever that we have here an authentic portrait of Lot's disobedient, though unfortunate wife. Ample and statuesque (as the salten image she was afterwards to become), the shawl-draped, masklike features are by no means beautiful. It is a face that you may often see to-day, in

[1] The Hon. ' Eddy ' Monteith had succumbed : the shock received by meeting a jackal while composing a sonnet had been too much for him. His tomb is in the Vale of Akko, beside the River Dis. Alas, for the *triste* obscurity of his end !

down-town 'Dancings,' or in the bars of the
dockyards, or wharfs, of our own modern
cities, Tilbury,' Frisco, Vera Cruz—a sodden,
gin-soaked face, that helps to vindicate, if
not, perhaps, excuse, the conduct of Lot. . . .
With this highly interesting example of the
Potters' Art, was found a novel object, of an
unknown nature, likely to arouse, in scientific
circles, considerable controversy. . . ."

And just as the lectrice was growing
hesitant, and embarrassed, the Countess of
Tolga, who had the *entrée*, unobtrusively
entered the room.

She was looking particularly well in one
of the new standing-out skirts ruched with
rosebuds, and was showing more of her
stockings than she usually did.

" You bring the sun with you ! " the
Queen graciously exclaimed.

" Indeed," the Countess answered, " I
ought to apologise for the interruption, but
the *poor little thing* is leaving now."

" What ? has the Abbess come ? "

" She has sent Sister Irene of the
Incarnation, instead. . . ."

" I had forgotten it was to-day."

With an innate aversion for all farewells, yet the Queen was accustomed to perform a score of irksome acts daily that she cordially disliked, and when, shortly afterwards, Mademoiselle de Nazianzi accompanied by a Sister from the Flaming-Hood were announced, they found her quite prepared.

Touched, and reassured at the ex-maid's appearance, the Queen judged, at last, it was safe to unbend. Already very remote and unworldly in her novice's dress, she had ceased, indeed, to be a being there was need any more to either circumvent, humour, or suppress ; and now that the threatened danger was gone, her Majesty glanced, half-lachrymosely, about among her personal belongings for some slight token of " esteem " or *souvenir*. Skimming from cabinet to cabinet, in a sort of hectic dance, she began to fear, as she passed her bibelots in review, that beyond a Chinese Buddha that she believed to be ill-omened, and which for a nun seemed hardly suitable, she could spare nothing about her after all, and in some dilemma, she raised her eyes, as though for a crucifix, towards the wall.

Above the long-chair a sombre study of a strangled negress in a ditch by Gauguin conjured up to-day with poignant force a vivid vision of the Tropics.

" The poor Duchess ! " she involuntarily sighed, going off into a train of speculation of her own.

Too tongue-tied, or, perhaps, too discreet, to inform the Queen that anything she might select would immediately be confiscated by the Abbess, Sister Irene, while professing her rosary, appraised her surroundings with furtive eyes, crossing herself frequently with a speed, and facility due to practice whenever her glance chanced to alight on some nude shape in stone. Keen, meagre, and perhaps slightly malicious, hers was a curiously pinched face—like a cold violet.

" The Abbess is still in retreat ; but sends her duty," she ventured as the Queen approached a gueridon near which she was standing.

" Indeed ? How I envy her," the Queen wistfully said, selecting, as suited to the requirements of the occasion, a little volume of a mystic trend, the *Cries of Love* of

THE FLOWER BENEATH THE FOOT

Father Surin,[1] bound in grey velvet, which she pressed upon the reluctant novice, with a brief, but cordial, kiss of farewell.

"She looked quite pretty!" she exclaimed, sinking to the long-chair as soon as the nuns had gone.

"So like the Cimabue in the long corridor . . ." the Countess of Tolga murmured chillily; It was her present policy that her adored ally, Olga Blumenghast, should benefit by Mademoiselle de Nazianzi's retirement from Court, by becoming nearer to the Queen, when they would work all the wires between them.

"I'd have willingly followed her," the Queen weariedly declared, "at any rate, until after the wedding."

"It seems that I and Lord Derbyfield are to share the same closed carriage in the wake of the bridal coach," the Countess of Tolga said, considering with a supercilious air her rose *suède* slipper on the dark carpet.

"He's like some great Bull. What do you suppose he talks about?"

The Countess d'Omptyda repressed a giggle.

[1] Author of *In the Dusk of the Dawn.*

"They tell me Don Juan was nothing *nothing* to him. . . . He cannot see, he cannot be, oh every hour. It seems he can't help it, and that he simply *has* to!"

"Fortunately Lady Lavinia Lee-Strange will be in the landau as well!"

The Queen laid her cheek to her hands.

"I all but died, dear Violet," she crooned, "listening to an account of her Ancestor, who fell, fighting Scotland, at the battle of Pinkie Cleugh."

"These well-bred, but detestably insular women, how they bore one."

"They are not to be appraised by any ordinary standards. Crossing the state saloon while coming here what should I see, ma'am, but Lady Canon of Noon on her hands and knees (all fours!) peeping below the loose-covers of the chairs in order to examine the Gobelins-tapestries beneath. . . ."

"Oh——"

"'Absolutely authentic' I said! as I passed on, leaving her looking like a pick-pocket caught in the act."

"I suppose she was told to make a quiet survey. . . ."

"Like their beagles and deer-hounds,

that their Landseer so loved to paint, I fear the British character is, at bottom, *nothing* if not rapacious ! "

" It's said, I believe, to behold the Englishman at his *best*, one should watch him play at tip-and-run."

" You mean of course at cricket ? "

The Queen looked doubtful : She had retained of a cricket-match at Lord's a memory of hatless giants waving wooden sticks.

" I only wish it could have been a long engagement," she abstrusely murmured, fastening her attention on the fountains whitely spurting in the gardens below.

Valets in cotton-jackets and light blue aprons bearing baskets of crockery and *argenterie*, were making ready beneath the tall Tuba trees, a supper *buffet* for the evening's Ball.

" Flap your wings, little bird
    O flap your wings——"

A lad's fresh voice, sweet as a robin's, came piping up.

" These   wretched   workpeople—— !
There's not a peaceful corner," the Queen complained,   as   her   husband's   shape

THE FLOWER BENEATH THE FOOT

appeared at the door.   He was followed by
his first secretary—a simple commoner,
yet, with the air, and manner, peculiar to
the husband of a Countess.

" Yes, Willie ? I've a hundred head-
aches.   What is it ? "

" Both King Geo and Queen Glory, are
wondering where you are."

" Oh, really, Willie ? "

" And dear Elsie's asking after you too."

" Very likely," the Queen returned with
quiet complaisance, " but unfortunately, I
have neither her energy, or," she murmured
with a slightly sardonic laugh, " her
appetite ! "

The Countess of Tolga tittered.

" She called for fried-eggs and butcher's-
meat, this morning, about the quarter
before eight," she averred.

" An excellent augury for our dynasty,"
the King declared, reposing the eyes of
an adoring grandparent upon an alabaster
head of a Boy attributed to Donatello.

" She's terribly foreign, Willie . . . !
Imagine ham and eggs . . ." the Queen
dropped her face to her hand.

" So long as the Royal-House——" The King broke off, turning gallantly to raise the Countess d'Omptyda, who had sunk with a gesture of exquisite allegiance to the floor.

" Sir . . . Sir ! " she faltered in confusion, seeking with fervent lips her Sovereign's hand.

" What is she doing, Willie ? "

" Begging for Strawberry-leaves ! " the Countess of Tolga brilliantly commented.

" Apropos of Honours . . . it appears King Geo has signified his intention of raising his present representative in Pisuerga to the peerage."

" After her recent *Cause*, Lady Something should be not a little consoled."

" She was at the début of the new diva, little Miss Hellvellyn (the foreign invasion has indeed begun !), at the Opera-House last night, so radiant. . . ."

" When she cranes forward out of her own box to smile at someone into the next, I can't explain . . . but one feels she ought to hatch," the Queen murmured, repairing capriciously from one couch to another.

" We neglect our guests, my dear," the

THE FLOWER BENEATH THE FOOT

King expostulatingly exclaimed, bending
over his consort anxiously from behind.

"Tell me, Willie," she cooed, caressing
the medals upon his breast, and drawing
him gently down: "tell me? Didst thou
enjoy thy cigar, dear, with King Geo?"

"I can recall in my time, Child, a suaver
flavour. . . ."

"Thy little chat, though, dearest, was
well enough?"

"I would not call him crafty, but I
should say he was a man of considerable
subtlety . . ." the King evasively replied.

"One does not need, my dearest
nectarine, a prodigy of intelligence however
to take him in!"

"Before the proposed Loan, love, can be
brought about, he may wish to question
thee as to thy political opinions."

The Queen gave a little light laugh.

"No one knows what my political
opinions are; I don't myself!"

"And I'm quite confident of it: But,
indeed, my dear, we neglect our functions."

"I only wish it could have been a *long*
engagement, Willie. . . ."

XV

IN the cloister eaves, the birds were just awakening, and all the spider scales, in the gargoyled gables, glanced fresh with dew. Above the Pietà, on the porter's gate, slow-speeding clouds, like knots of pink roses, came blowing across the sky, sailing away in titanic bouquets towards the clear horizon. All virginal in the early sunrise what enchantment the world possessed! The rhythmic sway-sway of the trees, the exhalations of the flowers, the ethereal candour of this early hour,— these raised the heart up to their Creator.

Kneeling at the casement of a postulant's cell, Laura de Nazianzi recalled that serene, and just thus had she often planned must dawn her bridal day!

Beyond the cruciform flower-beds, and the cloister wall, soared the Blue Jesus, the storied windows of its lofty galleries aglow with light.

THE FLOWER BENEATH THE FOOT

"Most gracious Jesus. Help me to forget. For my heart aches. Uphold me now."

But to forget to-day, was well-nigh she knew impossible. . . .

Once it seemed she caught the sound of splendid music from the direction of the Park, but it was too early for music yet. Away in the palace, the Princess Elsie must be already astir . . . in her peignoir, perhaps? The bridal-garment unfolded upon the bed: But no; it was said the bed indeed was where usually her Royal-Highness' dogs . . .

With a long and very involuntary sigh, she began to sweep, and put in some order, her room.

How forlorn her cornette looked upon her *prie-Dieu*! And, oh, how stern, and "old"!

Would an impulse to bend it slightly but only so, *so* slightly, to an angle to suit her face, be attended, later, by remorse?

"Confiteor Deo omnipotenti, beatae Mariae semper vergini, beato Michaeli Archangelo (et *tibi* Pater), quia peccavi nimis cogitatione, verbo et opere," she entreated, reposing her chin in meditation, upon the handle of her broom.

The bluish shadow of a cypress-tree, on the empty wall, fascinated her as few pictures had.

" Grant my soul Eyes," she prayed, cheerfully completing her task.

In the corridor, being a general holiday, all was yet quite still. A sound, as of gentle snoring, came indeed from behind more than one closed door, and the new *pensionnaire* was preparing to beat a retreat, when she perceived, in the cloister, the dumpish form of Old Jane.

Seated in the sun by the convent well, the Porteress was sharing a scrap of breakfast with the birds.

" You're soonish for Mass, love," she broke out, her large archaic features surcharged with smiles.

" It's such a perfect morning, I felt I must come down."

" I've seen many a more promising sunrise before now, my dear, turn to storm and blast ! An orange sky overhead,

brings back to me the morning that I was
received ; ah, I shall never forget, as I
was taking my Vows, a flash of forked
lightning, and a clap of Thunder (Glory
be to God !) followed by a water-spout
(Mercy save us !) bursting all over my
Frinch lace veil . . ."

" What is your book, Old Jane ? "

" Something light, love, as it's a holiday."

" *Pascal* . . ."

" Though it's mostly a *Fête* day I've
extra to do ! " the Porteress averred,
dropping her eyes to the great, glistening
spits, upon the Cloister flags. It was her
boast she could distinguish Monsignor
Potts' round splash from Father Geordie
Picpus' more dapper fine one, and again
the Abbess' from Mother Martinez de la
Rosa's—although these indeed shared a
certain opaque sameness.

" Of course it's a day for private visits."

" Since the affair of Sister Dorothea and
Brother Bernard Soult, private visits are
no longer allowed," the Porteress returned,
reproving modestly, with the cord of her
discipline, a pert little lizard, that seemed

to be proposing to penetrate between the nude toes of her sandalled foot.

But on such a radiant morning it was preposterous to hint at " Rules."

Beneath the clement sun a thousand cicadas were insouciantly chirping, while birds, skimming about without thoughts of money, floated lightly from tree to tree.

" Jesus—Mary—Joseph ! " the Porteress purred, as a Nun, with her face all muffled up in wool, crossed the Cloister, glancing neither to right nor left, and sharply slammed a door : for, already, the Convent was beginning to give signs of animation. Deep in a book of Our Lady's Hours, a biretta'd priest was slowly rounding a garden path, while repairing from a *Grotto-sepulchre*, to which was attached a handsome indulgence, Mother Martinez de la Rosa appeared, all heavily leaning on her stick.

Simultaneously the matins bell rang out, calling all to prayer.

The Convent Chapel founded by the tender enthusiasm of a wealthy widow, the Countess d'Acunha, to perpetuate her

THE FLOWER BENEATH THE FOOT

earthly comradeship with the beautiful Andalusian, the Doña Dolores Baatz, was still but thinly peopled some few minutes later, although the warning bell had stopped.

Peering around, Laura was disappointed not to remark Sister Ursula in her habitual place, between the veiled fresco of the "Circumcision" and the stoup of holy-water by the door.

Beyond an offer to "exchange whip-pings" there had been a certain coolness in the greeting with her friend, that had both surprised and pained her.

"When those we rely on wound and betray us, to whom should we turn but Thee?" she breathed, addressing a crucifix, in ivory, contrived by love, that was a miracle of wonder.

Finished Mass, there was a general rush for the Refectory!

Preceded by Sister Clothilde, and fol-lowed, helter-skelter, by an exuberant bevy of nuns, even Mother Martinez, who being shortsighted would go feeling the ground with her cane, was propelled to the measure of a hop-and-skip.

THE FLOWER BENEATH THE FOOT

Passing beneath an archway, labelled "Silence" (the injunction to-day being undoubtedly ignored), the company was welcomed by the mingled odours of tea, *consommé*, and fruit. It was a custom of the Convent for one of the Sisters during meal-time to read aloud from some standard work of fideism, and these edifying recitations, interspersed by such whispered questions as : "Tea, or *Consommé* ?" "A Banana, or a Pomegranate ?" gave to those at all foolishly, or hysterically inclined, a painful desire to giggle. Mounting the pulpit-lectern, a nun with an aristocratic, though gourmand little face, was about to resume the arid life of the Byzantine monk, Basilius Saturninus, when Mother Martinez de la Rosa took it upon herself, in a few patriotic words, to relax all rules for that day.

"We understand in the world now," a little faded woman murmured to Laura upon her right : "that the latest craze among ladies is to gild their tongues ; but I should be afraid," she added diffidently, dipping her banana into her tea, "of poison, myself ! "

214

THE FLOWER BENEATH THE FOOT

Unhappy at her friend's absence from the Refectory, Laura, however, was in no mood to entertain the nuns with stories of the present pagan tendencies of society.

Through the bare, blindless windows, framing a sky so bluely luminous, came the swelling clamour of the assembling crowds, tinging the languid air as with some sultry fever. From the *Chausée*, music of an extraordinary intention — heated music, crude music, played with passionate élan to perfect time, conjured up, with vivid, heartrending prosaicness, the seething Boulevards beyond the high old creeper-covered walls.

" I forget now, Mother, which of the Queens it is that will wear a velvet train of a beautiful orchid shade : But one of them will ! " Sister Irene of the Incarnation was holding forth.

" I must confess," Mother Martinez remarked, who was peeling herself a peach, with an air of far attention : " I must confess, I should have liked to have cast my eye upon the *lingerie* . . ."

" I would rather have seen the ball-wraps, Mother, or the shoes, and evening slippers ! "

" Yes, or the fabulous jewels . . ."

" Of course Sister Laura saw the *trousseau* ? "

But Laura made feint not to hear.

Discipline relaxed, a number of nuns had collected provisions and were picnicking in the window, where Sister Innez (an ex-Repertoire actress) was giving some spirited renderings of her chief successful parts — *Jane de Simerose, Frou-Frou, Sappho, Cigarette.* . . .

" My darling child ! I always sleep all day and only revive when there's *a Man*," she was saying with an impudent look, sending the• scandalised Sisters into delighted convulsions.

Unable to endure it any longer, Laura crept away.

A desire for air and solitude, led her towards the Recreation ground. After the hot refectory, sauntering in the silken shade of the old astounding cedars, was delightful quite. In the deserted alleys, the golden blossoms of the censia - trees, unable to resist the sun, littered in perfumed piles the ground, overcoming her before long with a sensation akin to *vertige*. Anxious to find her friend, Laura turned towards her cell.

She found Sister Ursula leaning on her window-ledge all crouched up — like a Duchess on " a First Night."

" My dear, my dear, the *crowds* ! "

" Ursula ? "

" Yes, what is it ? "

" Perhaps I'll go, since I'm in the way."

" Touchy Goose," Sister Ursula murmured wheeling round with a glance of complex sweetness.

" Ah, Ursula," Laura sighed, smiling reproachfully at her friend.

She had long almond eyes, one longer and larger than the other, that gave to her narrow, etiolated face, an exalted, mystic air. Her hair, wholly concealed by her full coif, would be inclined to rich copper or chestnut : Indeed, below the pinched and sensitive nostrils, a moustache (so slight as to be scarcely discernible) proved this beyond all controversy to be so. But perhaps the quality and beauty of her hands were her chief distinction.

" Do you believe it would cause an earthquake, if we climbed out, dear little one, upon the leads ? " she asked.

" I had forgotten you overlooked the street by leaning out," Laura answered, sinking fatigued to a little cane armchair.

" Listen, Laura . . . ! "

" This cheering racks my heart. . . ."

" Ah, Astaroth ! There went a very ' swell ' carriage."

" Perhaps I'll come back later : It's less noisy in my cell."

" Now you're here, I shall ask you, I think, to whip me."

" Oh, no. . . ."

" Bad dear Little-One. Dear meek soul," Sister Ursula softly laughed.

" This maddening cheering," Laura breathed, rolling tormented eyes about her.

A crucifix, a text : *I would lay Pansies at Jesus' Feet*, two fresh eggs in a blue paper bag, some ends of string, a breviary, and a birch, were the chamber's individual, if meagre, contents.

THE FLOWER BENEATH THE FOOT

" You used *not* to have that text, Ursula,"
Laura observed, her attention arrested by
the preparation of a Cinematograph Company on the parapet of the Cathedral.

The Church had much need indeed of
Reformation ! The Times were incredibly
low : A new crusade . . . she ruminated,
revolted at the sight of an old man holding dizzily to a stone-winged angel, with
a wine-flask at his lips.

" Come, dear, won't you assist me now
to mortify my senses ? " Sister Ursula
cajoled.

" No, really, no— !— !— ! "

" Quite lightly : For I was scourged, by
Sister Agnes, but yesterday, with a heavy
bunch of keys, head downwards, hanging
from a bar."

" Oh . . ."

" This morning she sent me those pullets'
eggs. I perfectly was touched by her
delicate sweet sympathy."

Laura gasped.

" It must have hurt you ? "

" I assure you I felt nothing—my spirit
had travelled so far," Sister Ursula replied,

turning to throw an interested glance at the street.

It was close now upon the critical hour, and the plaudits of the crowd were becoming more and more uproarious, as "favourites" in Public life, and "celebrities" of all sorts, began to arrive in brisk succession at the allotted door of the Cathedral.

" I could almost envy the fleas in the Cardinal's vestments," Sister Ursula declared, overcome by the venal desire to see.

Gazing at the friend upon whom she had counted in some disillusion, Laura quietly left her.

The impulse to witness something of the spectacle outside was, nevertheless, infectious, and recollecting that from the grotto-sepulchre in the garden it was not impossible to attain the convent wall, she determined, moved by some wayward instinct, to do so. Frequently, as a child, had she scaled it, to survey the doings of the city streets beyond—the streets, named by the nuns often "Sinward-ho." Crossing the cloisters, and through old gates crowned by vast fruit-baskets in stone, she followed,

220

feverishly ,the ivy - masked bricks of the
sheltering wall, and was relieved to reach
the grotto without encountering anyone.
Surrounded by heavy boskage, it marked
a spot where, once, long ago, one of the
Sisters, it was said, had received the
mystic stigmata. . . . With a feline effort
(her feet supported by the Grotto boulders),
it needed but a bound to attain an incomparable post of vantage.

Beneath a blaze of bunting, the street
seemed paved with heads. " Madonna,"
she breathed, as an official on a white
horse, its mane stained black, began
authoritatively backing his steed into the
patient faces of the mob, startling an infant
in arms below, to a frantic fit of squalls.

" Just so shall we stand on the Day of
Judgment," she reflected, blinking at the
glare.

Street boys vending programmes,
'Lucky' horseshoes, Saturnalian emblems
—(these for gentlemen only), offering post-
cards of ' Geo and Glory,' etc., wedged their
way however where it might have been
deemed indeed impossible for anyone to pass.

And *he*, she wondered, her eyes following the wheeling pigeons, alarmed by the recurrent salutes of the signal guns, he must be there already: Under the dome! Restive a little beneath the busy scrutiny, his tongue like the point of a blade . . .

A burst of cheering seemed to announce the Queen. But no, it was only a lady, with a parasol sewn with diamonds, that was exciting the rah-rahs of the crowd. Followed by mingled cries of " Shame ! " " Waste ! " and sighs of envy, Madame Wetme was enjoying a belated triumph. And now a brief lull, as a brake containing various delegates and " representatives of English Culture," rolled by at a stately trot—Lady Alexander, E. V. Lucas, Robert Hichens, Clutton Brock, etc.,—the ensemble the very apotheosis of worn-out *cliché*.

" There's someone there wot's got enough heron plumes on her head ! " a young girl in the crowd remarked.

And nobody contradicted her.

Then troops and outriders, and at last the Queen.

She was looking charming in a Corinthian

chlamyde, in a carriage lined in deep delphinium blue, behind six restive blue roan horses.

Finally, the bride and her father, bowing this way and that . . .

Cheers.

" Huzzas "—

A hushed suspense.

Below the wall the voice of a beggar arose, persistent, haunting : " For the Love of God . . . In the Name of Pity . . . of Pity.

" Of Pity," she echoed, addressing a frail, wind-sown harebell, blue as the sky : And leaning upon the shattered glass ends, that crowned the wall, she fell to considering the future—Obedience, Solitude— death.

The troubling *valse* theme from *Dante in Paris* interrupted her meditations.

How often had they valsed it together, he and she . . . sometimes as a two-step . . . ! What souvenirs. . . . Yousef, Yousef. . . . Above the Cathedral, the crumbling clouds, had eclipsed the sun. In the intense meridian glare the thronged

street seemed even as though half-hyp-
notised; occasionally only the angle of a
parasol would change, or some bored
soldier's legs would give a little. When
brusquely, from the belfry, burst a
triumphant clash of bells.

Laura caught her breath.

Already?

A shaking of countless handkerchiefs in
wild ovation : From roof-tops, and balconies,
the air was thick with falling flowers—the
bridal pair !

But only for the bridegroom had she eyes.

Oblivious of what she did, she began to
beat her hands, until they streamed with
blood, against the broken glass ends upon
the wall: " Yousef, Yousef, Yousef. . . ."

July 1921, *May* 1922.
Versailles, Montreux, Florence.

Prancing Nigger

I

LOOKING gloriously bored, Miss Miami Mouth gaped up into the boughs of a giant silk-cotton tree. In the lethargic noontide nothing stirred: all was so still, indeed, that the sound of someone snoring was clearly audible among the cane-fields far away.

" After dose yams an' pods an' de white falernum, I dats way sleepy too," she murmured, fixing heavy, somnolent, eyes upon the prospect that lay before her.

Through the sun-tinged greenery shone the sea, like a floor of silver glass strewn with white sails.

Somewhere out there, fishing, must be her boy, Bamboo!

And, inconsequently, her thoughts wandered from the numerous shark-casualties of late to the mundane proclivities of her mother; for to quit the little village of

Mediavilla for the capital was that dame's fixed obsession.

Leave Mediavilla, leave Bamboo! The young negress fetched a sigh.

In what, she reflected, way would the family gain by *entering society*, and how did one enter it, at all? There would be a gathering, doubtless, of the elect (probably armed), since the best society is exclusive, and difficult to enter. And, then? Did one burrow? Or charge? She had sometimes heard it said that people " pushed " . . . and closing her eyes, Miss Miami Mouth sought to picture her parents, assisted by her small sister, Edna, and her brother, Charlie, forcing their way, perspiring, but triumphant, into the highest social circles of the city of Cuna-Cuna.

Across the dark Savannah country the city lay, one of the chief alluring cities of the world: The Celestial city of Cuna-Cuna, Cuna, city of Mimosa, Cuna, city of Arches, Queen of the Tropics, Paradise — almost invariably travellers referred to it like that.

Oh, everything must be fantastic there, where even the very pickneys put on clothes!

And Miss Miami Mouth glanced fondly down at her own plump little person, nude, but for a girdle of creepers that she would gather freshly twice a day.

" It would be a shame, sh'o, to cover it," she murmured drowsily, caressing her body, and smiling up into the blue absolute of the sky, and moved to a sudden spasm of laughter, she tittered: " No! really. De ideah!"

II

"SILVER bean-stalks, silver bean-stalks, oh hé, oh hé," down the long village street, from door to door, the cry repeatedly came, until the vendor's voice was lost on the evening air.

In a rocking chair, before the threshold of a palm thatched cabin, a matron with broad, bland features, and a big, untidy figure, surveyed the scene with a nonchalant eye.

Beneath some tall trees, bearing flowers like flaming bells, a few staid villagers sat enjoying the rosy dusk, while, strolling towards the sea, two young men passed by with fingers intermingled.

With a slight shrug, the lady plied her fan.

As the Mother of a pair of oncoming girls, the number of ineligible young men, or confirmed *bachelors* around the neighbourhood was a constant source of irritation. . . .

" Sh'o, dis remoteness bore an' weary me to death," she exclaimed, addressing some-one through the window behind; and receiv-ing no audible answer, she presently rose, and went within.

It was the hour when, fortified by a siesta, Mrs. Ahmadou Mouth was wont to ap-proach her husband on general household affairs, and to discuss, in particular, the question of their removal to the town; for, with the celebration of their Pearl-wedding, close at hand, the opportunity to make the announcement of a change of residence to their guests, ought not, she believed, to be missed.

" We leave Mediavilla for de education ob my daughters," she would say; or, per-haps: " We go to Cuna-Cuna, for de fin-ishing ob *mes filles!* "

But, unfortunately, the reluctance of Mr. Mouth to forsake his Home, seemed to increase from day to day.

She found him asleep, bolt upright, his head gently nodding, beneath a straw-hat beautifully browned.

" Say, nigger, lub," she murmured,

brushing her hand featheringly along his knee, " say, nigger, lub, I gotta go! "

It was the tender prelude to the storm.

Evasive, (and but half-awake), he warned her. " Let me alone; Ah'm thinkin'."

" Prancing nigger, now come on! "

" Ah'm thinkin'."

" Tell me what for dis procrastination? " Exasperated, she gripped his arm.

But for all reply, Mr. Mouth drew a volume of revival hymns towards him, and turned on his wife his back.

" You ought to shame o' you-self, sh'o," she caustically commented, crossing to the window.

The wafted odours of the cotton trees without, oppressed the air. In the deepening twilight, the rising moonmist, already obscured the street.

" Dis place not healthy. Dat damp! Should my daughters go off into a decline . . ." she apprehensively murmured, as her husband started softly to sing.

> "For ebber wid de Lord!
> Amen; so let it be
> Life from de dead is in dat word
> 'Tis immortality."

PRANCING NIGGER

" If it's de meeting-house dats de ob-
struction, dair are odders, too, in Cuna-
Cuna,'' she observed.

" How often hab I bid you nebba to mention dat modern Sodom in de hearing ob my
presence! ''

" De Debil frequent de village, fo' dat
matter, besides de town.''

" Sh'o nuff.''

" But yestiddy, dat po' silly negress
Ottalie was seduced again in a Mango
track — ; an' dats de third time! ''

> " Heah in de body pent,
> Absent from Him I roam
> Yet nightly pitch my movin' tent
> A day's march nearer home."

" Prancing nigger, from dis indifference
to your fambly, be careful lest you do
arouse de vials ob de Lord's wrath! ''

" Yet nightly pitch — '' he was beginning again, in a more subdued key, but the
tones of his wife arrested him.

" Prancing Nigger, lemme say sumptin'
more! '' Mrs. Mouth took a long sighing
breath: " In dis dark jungle my lil jewel
Edna, I feah, will wilt away. . . .''

234

" Wh'a gib you cause to speak like dat ? "

" I was tellin' my fortune lately wid de cards," she reticently made reply, insinuating, by her half-turned eyes, that more disclosures of an ominous nature concerning others besides her daughter had been revealed to her as well.

" Lordey Lord; what is it den you want ? "

" I want a Villa with a watercloset — " flinging wiles to the winds, it was a cry from the heart.

" De Lord hab pity on dese vanities an' innovations ! "

" In town, you must rememba, often de houses are far away from de parks; — de city, in dat respect, not like heah."

" Say nothin' more ! De widow ob my po' brudder Willie, across de glen, she warn me I ought nebba to listen to you."

" Who care for a common woman, dat only read de ' Negro World,' an' nebba see anyt'ing else ! " she swelled.

Mr. Mouth turned conciliatingly.

" To-morrow, me arrange for de victuals for our ebenin' at Home ! "

" Good, bery fine," she murmured, acknowledging through the window the cordial " good-night " of a few late labourers, returning from the fields, each with a bundle of sugar-cane poised upon the head.

" As soon as marnin' dawn me take dis bizniz in hand."

" Only pramas, nigger darlin'," she cajoled, " dat durin' de course ob de reception, you make a lil speech to inform de neighbours ob our gwine away bery soon, for de sake of de education ob our girls."

" Ah cyan pramas nothing'."

" I could do wid a change too, honey, after my last miscarriage."

" Change come wid our dissolution," he assured her, " quite soon enuff! "

" Bah," she murmured, rubbing her cheek to his: " we set out on our journey sh'o in de season ob Novemba."

To which with asperity he replied: " *Not for two Revolutions!* " and rising brusquely, strode solemnly from the room.

" Hey-do-day," she yawned, starting a wheezy gramophone, and sinking down upon his empty chair; and she was lost in ball-room fancies, (whirling in the arms of some blonde young foreigner), when she caught sight of her daughter's reflection in the glass.

Having broken, or discarded her girdle of leaves, Miss Miami Mouth, attracted by the gramophone, appeared to be teaching a hectic two-step to the cat.

" Fie, fie, my lass. Why you be so *Indian?* " her mother exclaimed, bestowing with the full force of a carpet-slipper, a well-aimed spank from behind.

" *Aïe, aïe!* "

" Sh'o: you nohow select! "

" *Aïe. . . .* "

" De low exhibition! "

" I had to take off my apron, 'cos it seemed to draw de bees," Miami tearfully explained, catching up the cat in her arms.

" Ob course, if you choose to wear roses. . . ."

" It was but ivy! "

" De berries ob de ivy, entice de same," Mrs. Mouth replied, nodding graciously, from the window, to Papy Paul, the next door neighbour, who appeared to be taking a lonely stroll with a lanthorn and a pine-apple.

" I dats way wondering why Bamboo, no pass, dis ebenin', too; as a rule, it is seldom he stop so late out upon de sea," the young girl ventured.

" After I shall introduce you to de world, (de advantage ob a good marriage; when I t'ink ob mine!), you will be ashamed, sh'o, to recall dis infatuation."

" De young men ob Cuna-Cuna, (tell me, Mammee), are dey den so nice? "

" Ah, Chile! If I was your age again . . ."

" Sh'o, dair's nothin' so much in dat."

" As a young girl of eight, (Tee-hee!) I was distracting to all the gentlemen," Mrs. Mouth asserted, confiding a smile to a small, long-billed bird, in a cage, of the variety known as Bequia-Sweet.

" How I wish I'd been born, like you, in August-Town, across de Isthmus! "

" It gib me dis taste fo' S'ciety, Chile."

" In S'cieyt, don't dey dress wid clothes on ebery day? "

" Sh'o; surtainly."

" An' don't dey nebba tickle ? "

" In August-Town, de aristocracy conceal de best part ob deir bodies; not like heah! "

" An' tell me, Mammee . . . ? De first lover you eber had . . . was he half as handsome as Bamboo ? "

" De first dude, Chile, I eber had, was a lil, lil buoy, . . . wid no hair (whatsoeber at all,) bal' like a calabash! " Mrs. Mouth replied, as her daughter Edna entered with the lamp.

" Frtt! " the wild thing tittered, setting it down with a bang: with her cincture of leaves and flowers, she had the éclat of a butterfly.

" Better fetch de shade," Mrs. Mouth exclaimed, staring squeamishly at Miami's shadow on the wall.

" Already it grow dark; no one about now at dis hour ob night at all."

" Except thieves an' ghouls," Mrs. Mouth replied, her glance straying towards the window.

But only the little blue winged Bats were passing beneath a fairyland of stars.

"When I do dis, or dis, my shadow appear as formed as Mimi's!"

"Sh'o, Edna, she dat provocative today."

"Be off at once Chile, an' lay de table for de ebenin' meal; an' be careful not to knock de shine off de new tin-teacups," Mrs. Mouth commanded, taking up an Estate-Agent's catalogue, and seating herself comfortably beneath the lamp.

"'City of Cuna-Cuna,'" she read, "'*in the Heart of a Brainy District,* (within easy reach of University, shops, etc.) A charming, Freehold Villa. Main drainage. Extensive views. Electric light. Every convenience.'"

"Dat sound just de sort ob lil shack for me."

III

THE strange sadness of evening, the détresse of the Evening Sky! Cry, cry white Rain Birds out of the West, cry . . . !

" An' so, Miami, you no come back no more? "

" No, no come back."

Flaunting her boredom by the edge of the sea one close of day, she had chanced to fall in with Bamboo, who, stretched at length upon the beach, was engaged in mending a broken net.

" An' I dats way glad," she half-resentfully pouted, jealous a little of his toil.

But, presuming deafness, the young man laboured on, since, to support an aged mother, and to attain one's desires, perforce necessitates work; and his fondest wish, by dint of saving, was to wear on his wedding-day a pink starched cotton shirt — a starched, pink cotton shirt, stiff as a boat's-sail when the North winds caught it!

But a pink shirt would mean trousers . . .
and trousers would lead to shoes . . .
" Extravagant nigger, don't you dare! " he
would exclaim, in dizzy panic, from time to
time, aloud.

" Forgib me, honey," he begged, " but
me obliged to finish, while de daylight last."

" Sh'o," she sulked, following the amazing strategy of the sunset-clouds.

" Miami angel you look so sweet: I dat
amorous ob you, Mimi! "

A light laugh tripped over her lips:

" Say buoy, how you getting on? " she
queried, sinking down on her knees beside
him.

" I dat amorous ob you! "

" Oh, ki," she tittered, with a swift mocking glance at his crimson loincloth. She
had often longed to snatch it away.

" Say you lub me, just a lil, too, deah? "

" Sh'o," she answered softly, sliding over
on to her stomach, and laying her cheek to
the flats of her hands.

Boats with crimson spouts, to wit, steam-
ers, dotted the skyline far away, and
barques, with sails like the wings of butter-

flies, borne by an idle breeze, were bringing
more than one ineligible young mariner,
back to the prose of shore.

" Ob wha' you t'inking? "

" Nothin', she sighed, contemplating laconically a little transparent shell of violet
pearl, full of sea-water and grains of sand,
that the wind ruffled as it blew.

" Not ob *any* sort ob lil t'ing? " he caress-
ingly insisted, breaking an open dark flower
from her belt of wild Pansy.

" I should be gwine home," she breathed,
recollecting the undoing of the negress
Ottalie.

" Oh, I dat amorous ob you, Mimi."

" If you want to finish dat net, while de
daylight last."

For oceanward, in a glowing ball, the sun
had dropped already.

" Sh'o, nigger, I only wish to be kind,"
she murmured, getting up, and sauntering a
few paces along the strand.

Lured, perhaps, by the nocturnal phos-
phorescence from its lair, a water-scorpion,
disquieted at her approach, turned and
vanished amid the sheltering cover of the

rocks. " Isht, isht," she squealed, wading after it into the surf; but to find it, look as she would, was impossible. Dark, curious and anxious, in the fast failing light, the sea disquieted her too, and it was consoling to hear close behind her, the solicitous voice of Bamboo.

" Us had best soon be movin', befo' de murk ob night."

The few thatched cabins, that comprised the village of Mediaville, lay not half-a-mile from the shore. Situated between the savannah and the sea, on the southern side of the island known as Tacarigua, (the " burning Tacarigua " of the Poets), its inhabitants were obliged, from lack of communication with the larger island centres, to rely to a considerable extent for a livelihood among themselves. Local market-days, held, alternatively, at Valley Village, or Broken Hill (the nearest approach to industrial towns in the district around Mediavilla, were the chief source of rural trade, when such merchandise as fish, coral, beads, bananas and loincloths, would exchange hands amid much animation, social gossip and pleasant fun.

" Wh'a you say to dis? " she queried, as they turned inland through the cane-fields, holding up a fetish known as a " luck-ball," attached to her throat by a chain.

" Who gib it you? " he shortly demanded, with a quick suspicious glance.

" Mammee, she bring it from Valley Village, an' she bring another for my lil sister, too."

" Folks say she attend de Market only to meet de Obi man, who cast a spell so dat your Dada move to Cuna-Cuna."

" Dat so! "

" Your Mammee no seek ebber de influence of Obeah? "

" Not dat I know ob! " she replied; nevertheless, she could not but recall her mother's peculiar behaviour of late, especially upon Market days, when instead of conversing with her friends, she would take herself off, with a mysterious air, saying she was going to the Baptist Chapel.

" Mammee, she hab no faith in de Witch-Doctor, at all," she murmured, halting to lend an ear to the liquid note of a Pea-dove among the canes.

"I no care; me follow after wherebber you go," he said, stealing an arm about her.

"True?" she breathed, looking up languidly towards the white mounting moon.

"I dat amorous ob you, Mimi."

IV

IT WAS the Feast night. In the grey spleen of evening through the dusty lanes towards Mediavilla, county-society flocked.

Peering round a cow-shed door, Primrose and Phoebe, procured as waitresses for the occasion, felt their valour ooze as they surveyed the arriving guests, and dropping prostrate amid the straw declared, in each others arms, that never, never would they find the courage to appear.

In the road, before a tall tamarind tree, a well-spread supper board exhaled a pungent odour of fried cascadura fish, exciting the plaintive ravings of the wan pariah dogs, and the cries of a few little stark naked children engaged as guardians to keep them away. Defying an ancient and inelegant custom, by which the hosts welcomed their guests by the side of the road, Mrs. Mouth had elected to remain within the precincts of the house, where, according to tradition, the bridal trophies, cowrie-shells, feathers, and a bouquet of faded orange blossom,— were being displayed.

" It seem no more dan yestidday," she was holding forth gaily over a goblet of Sangaree wine, " it seem no more dan yes-tidday dat I put on me maiden wreath ob arange blastams to walk wid me nigger to church."

Clad in rich-hued creepers, she was both looking and feeling her best.

" Sh'o," a woman with blonde-dyed hair and Buddery eyes exclaimed, " it seem no more dan just like yestidday; dat not so, Papy Paul? " she queried, turning to an old man in a raspberry-pink kerchief, who displayed, (as he sat) more of his person than he seemed to be aware of.

But Papy Paul was confiding a receipt for pickling yuccas to Mamma Luna, the mother of Bamboo, and made as if not to hear.

Offering a light, lilac wine, sweet and heady, Miami circled, here and there. She had a cincture of white rose-oleanders, and

PRANCING NIGGER

a bandeau of blue convolvoli. She held a
fan.

"Or do you care for anyt'ing else?"
she was enquiring, automatically, of Mr.
Musket, (the Father of three very common
girls), as a melodious tinkle of strings announced the advent of the minstrels from
Broken Hill.

Following the exodus roadward, it was
agreeable to reach the outer air.

Under the high trees by the yard-door
gate, the array of vehicles and browsing
quadrupeds, was almost as numerous as
upon a market-day. Coming and going between the little Café of the "Forty Par-
rots" (with its Bar, spelled *Biar* in twinkling lights), the quiet village road was agog,
with bustling folk, as perhaps never before.
All iris in the dusk, a few loosely-loin-
clothed young men, had commenced dancing
aloofly among themselves, bringing down
some light (if bitter) banter, from the
belles.

Pirouetting with these, Miami recognized
the twinkling feet of her brother Charlie, a
lad who preferred roaming the wide savan-

nah country after butterflies with his net, to the ever increasing etiquette of his home.

"Sh'o, S'ciety no longer what it wa'," the mother of two spare lean girls, like young giraffes, was lamenting, when a clamorous gong summoned the assembly to the festal board.

In the glow of blazing palm logs, stoked by capering pickneys, the company, with some considerable jostling, became seated by degrees.

"Fo' what we gwine to recebe, de Lord make us to be truly t'ankful," Mr. Mouth's low voice was lost amid the din. Bending to the decree of Providence, and trusting in God for the welfare of his house, he was resigned to follow the call of duty, by allowing his offspring such educational advantages and worldly polish, that only a city can give.

"An' so I heah you gwine to leab us!" the lady at his elbow exclaimed, helping herself to a claw of a crab.

"Fo' de sake ob de chillens schoolin'," Mr. Mouth made reply, blinking at the brisk lightning play through the foliage of the trees.

" Dey tell me de amount of licence dat go on ober dah," she murmured, indicating with her claw the chequered horizon, " but de whole world needs revising, as de Missionary truly say!"

" Indeed, an' dats de trute."

" It made me cry," a plump little woman declared, " when de Minister speak so serious, out ob de pulpit, on de skangle ob close dancing. . . ."

" Fo' one t'ing lead sh'o to de nex'! " Mr. Mouth obstrusely assented, turning his attention upon an old negress answering to the name of Mamma May, who was retailing how she had obtained the sunshade, beneath which, since noon, she had walked all the way to the party.

" Ah could not afford a parasol, so Ah just cut miself a l'il green bush, an' held it up ober my head," she was crooning in gleeful triumph.

" It's a wonder, indeed, no one gib you a lif'! " several voices observed, but the discussion was drowned by an esoteric song of remote, tribal times, from the lips of Papy Paul.

PRANCING NIGGER

" I am King Elephant-bag,
Ob de rose-pink Mountains!
Tatou, tatouay, tatou. . . ."

provoking a giggle from Miss Stella
Spooner, the marvellous daughter of an
elderly father, and, in which, she was
joined, by the youngest Miss Mouth.

Incontestably a budding Princess, the
playful mite was enjoying, with airy nonchalance, her initial experience of Society.

" Ob course she is very *jeune*," Mrs.
Mouth murmured archly, behind her hand,
into the ear of Mr. Musket.

" It's de Lord's will," he cautiously replied, rolling a mystified eye towards his
wife, (a sable negress out of Africa), continually vaunting her foreign extraction:
" I'm Irish," she would say: " I'm Irish,
deah. . . ."

" Sh'o she de born image ob her elder
sister! "

" De world all say she to marry de son
ob ole Mamma Luna, dat keep de lil shop."

" Suz! Wha' nex'? " Mrs. Mouth returned, breaking off to focus Papy Paul,
apparently, already, far from sober: " I

hav' saw God, an' I hav' spoke wid de President, too!'' he was announcing impressively to Mamma Luna, a little old woman in whose veins ran the blood of many races.

'' Dair's no trute at all in *dat* report,'' Mrs. Mouth quietly added, signalling direction to a sturdy, round-bottomed little lad, who had undertaken to fill the gap caused by Primrose and Phoebe.

Bearing a panier piled with fruit, he had not got far before the minstrels called forth several couples to their feet.

The latest jazz, bewildering, glittering, exuberant as the soil, a jazz, throbbing, pulsating, with a zim, zim, zim, a jazz all abandon and verve that had drifted over the glowing savannah and the waving canefields from Cuna-Cuna by the Violet Sea, invited, irresistibly, to motion, every boy and girl.

'' Prancing nigger, hab a dance?'' his wife, transported, shrilled: but Mr. Mouth was predicting a Banana slump, to Mrs. Walker, the local midwife, and paid no heed.

Torso-to-torso, the youngsters twirled, while even a pair of majestic matrons, Mrs. Friendship and Mrs. Mother, went whirling away, (together), into the brave summer dusk. Accepting the invitation of Bamboo, Miami rose, but before dancing long complained of the heat.

" Sh'o, it cooler in de Plantation," he suggested, pointing along the road.

" Oh, I too much afraid! "

" What for you afraid? "

But Miami only laughed, and tossed her hand as if she were scattering dewdrops.

Following the roving fireflies, and the adventurous flittermice, they strolled along in silence. By the roadside, two young men, friends, walking with fingers intermingled, saluted them softly. An admirable evening for a promenade! Indescribably sweet, the floating field-scents, enticed them witchingly on.

" Shi! " she exclaimed as a bird skimmed swiftly past with a chattering cry.

" It noddin', deah, but a lil wee owl! "

" An' it to make my heart go so," she murmured, with a side-long smiling glance.

He had a new crimson loincloth, and a blood pink carnation at his ear.

" What for you afraid? " he tenderly pressed.

" It much cooler heah, doh it still very hot," she inconsequently answered, pausing to listen to the fretting of the hammer-tree-frogs in the dusk.

" Dey hold a concert honey lub, all for us."

Rig a jig jig, rig a jig jig. . . .

" Just hark to de noise! " she murmured, starting a little at the silver lightning behind the palms.

" Just hark," he repeated, troubled.

Rig a jig jig, rig a jig jig. . . .

V

LITTLE jingley trot-trot-trot, over the Savannah, hey — !

Joggling along towards Cuna-Cuna the creaking caravan shaped its course. Seated in a hooded chariot, berced by mule-bells, and nibbling a shoot of ripe cane, Mrs. Mouth appeared to have attained the heights of bliss. Disregarding, or insensitive to her husband's incessant groans, (wedged in between a case of pineapples, and a box marked " lingerie "), she abandoned herself voluptuously to her thoughts. It was droll to contemplate meeting an old acquaintance, Nini Snagg, who had gone to reside in Cuna-Cuna long ago: " Fancy seein' you! " she would say, and how they both would laugh.

Replying tersely to the innumerable " what would you do ifs " of her sister, supposing attacks from masked-bandits or ferocious wild-animals, Miami moped.

All her whole heart yearned back behind
her and never had she loved Bamboo so
much as now.

" — if a big, shaggy buffalo, wid two,
sharp, horns, dat long, were to rush right at
you ? " Edna was plaguing her, when a sudden jolt of the van set up a loud cackling
from a dozen scared cocks and hens.

" Drat dose fowl; as if dair were none
in Cuna-Cuna! " Mrs. Mouth addressed her
husband.

" Not birds ob dat brood," he retorted,
plaintively starting to sing.

" I t'ink when I read dat sweet story ob old,
  When Jesus was here among men,
  How He called lil chillens as lambs to His fold,
  I should hab like to hab been wid dem den!
  I wish dat His hands had been placed ahn my
    head,
  Dat His arms had been thrown aroun' me,
  An' dat I might hab seen His kind look when
    He said,
  Let de lil ones come unto Me! "

" Mind de dress-basket, don't drop down,
deah, an' spoil our clo'," Mrs. Mouth exclaimed, indicating a cowskin trunk that

seemed to be in peril of falling; for, from
motives of economy and ease, it had been
decided that, not before Cuna-Cuna should
rear her queenly towers above them, would
they change their floral garlands for the
more artificial fabrics of the town, and,
when Edna, vastly to her importance,
should go into a pair of frilled " invisibles "
and a petticoat for the first amazing time;
nor, indeed, would Mr. Mouth himself take
" to de pants," until his wife and daughters
should have assumed their skirts.   But this,
from the languid pace at which their ve-
hicle proceeded, was unlikely to be just yet.
In the torrid tropic noontime, haste however was quite out of the question.   Bordered by hills, long, yellow and low, the
wooded savannah rolled away beneath a
blaze of trembling heat.

" I don't t'ink much ob dis part of de
country," Mrs. Mouth commented.   " All
dese common palms . . . de cedar wood
tree, dat my tree.   Dat is de timber I
prefer."

" An' some," Edna pertly smiled, " **dey**
like best de bamboo. . . ."

A remark that was rewarded by a blow on the ear.

"Now she set up a hullabaloo like de time de scorpion bit her botty," Mrs. Mouth lamented, and, indeed, the uproar made, alarmed from the boskage a cloud of winsome soldier-birds and inquisitive parroquets.

"Oh my God," Mr. Mouth exclaimed. "What for you make all dat dere noise?" But his daughter paid no attention, and soon sobbed herself to sleep.

Advancing through tracks of acacia-scrub, or groves of nutmeg-trees, they jolted along in the gay, exalting sunlight. Flowers brighter than love wafting the odour of spices, strewed in profusion the long guinea-grass on either side of the way.

"All dose sweet aprons, if it weren't fo' de flies!" Mrs. Mouth murmured, regarding some heavy, ambered, Trumpet flowers, with a covetous eye.

"I trust Charlie get bit by no snake!"

"Prancing Nigger! It a lil too late now to t'ink ob dat."

Since to avoid overcrowding the family

party, Charlie was to follow with his butterfly net, and arrive as he could. And never
were butterflies, (seen in nigger-boys
dreams) as brilliant, or frolicsome, as were
those of mid-savannah-Azure Soledads, and
radiant Conquistadors with frail flamboyant wings, wove about the labouring mules
perpetual fresh rosettes.

"De Lord protect de lad," Mr. Mouth
remarked, relapsing into silence.

Onward through the cloudless noontide,
beneath the ardent sun, the caravan, drowsily crawled. As the afternoon advanced,
Mrs. Mouth produced a pack of well
thumbed cards, and cutting, casually, twice,
began interrogating Destiny with these.
Reposing as best she might, Miami gave
herself up to her reflections. The familiar
aspect of the wayside palms, the tattered
pennons of the bananas, the big silk-cottons,
(known, to children, as 'Mammee-trees'),
all brought to her mind Bamboo.

"Dair's somet'in' dat look like a death
dah, at's troublin' me," Mrs. Mouth remarked, moodily fingering a greasy ace.

" De Almighty forgib dese foolish games! " Mr. Mouth protestingly said.

" An' from de lie ob de cards . . . it seem as ef de corpse were ob de masculine species."

" Wha' gib you de notion ob dat? "

" Sh'o, a sheep puts his wool on his favourite places," Mrs. Mouth returned, reshuffling slowly her pack.

Awakened by her Father's psalms, Edna's " What would you do's " had commenced with volubility anew, growing more eerie with the gathering night.

" . . . if a Wood-Sprit wid two heads an' six arms, were to take hold ob you, Miami, from behind? "

" I no do nothin' at all," Miami answered briefly.

" Talk not so much ob de jumbies, chile, as de chickens go to roost! " Mrs. Mouth admonished.

" Or, if de debil himself should? " Edna insisted, allowing Snowball, the cat, to climb on to her knee.

" Nothin', sh'o," Miami murmured, regarding dreamily the sun's sinking disk, that was illuminating all the Western sky with incarnadine and flamingo-rose. Ominous in the falling dusk, the savannah rolled away, its radiant hues effaced beneath a rapid tide of deepening shadow.

" Start de gramophone gwine girls, an' gib us somet'in' bright! " Mrs. Mouth exclaimed, depressed by the forlorn note of the Twa-oo-Twa-oo bird, that mingled its lament with a thousand night cries from the grass.

" When de saucy female sing: ' My Ice Cream Girl,' fo' sh'o she scare de elves."

And as though by force of magic, the nasal soprano of an invisible songstress rattled forth with tinkling gusto a music-hall air with a sparkling refrain.

> " And the boys shout Girlie, hi!
> Bring me soda, soda, soda,
> (Aside, spoken) (Stop your fooling there and
>   let me alone!)
> For I'm an Ice Cream Soda
>   Girl."

" It put me in mind ob de last sugar-factory explosion! It was de same day dat

Snowball crack de Tezzrazine record. Drat de cat.''

"O, Lordey Lord! Wha' for you make dat din?" Mr. Mouth complained, knotting a cotton handkerchief over his head.

"I hope you not gwine to be billeous honey, afore we get to Lucia?"

"Lemme alone. Ah'm thinkin'. . . .''

Pressing on by the light of a large clear moon, the hamlet of Lucia, the halting-place proposed for the night, lay still far ahead.

Stars, like many Indian pinks, flecked with pale brightness the sky above; towards the horizon shone the Southern Cross, while the Pole Star, through the palm-fronds, came and went.

> *And the men cry Girlie, hi!*
> *Bring me* —

"Silence, dah! Ah'm thinkin' . . .''

VI

CUNA, full of charming roses, full of violet shadows, full of music, full of Love, Cuna . . . !

Leaning from a balcony of the Grand Savannah hotel, their instincts all aroused, Miami and Edna gazed out across the Alemeda, a place all foliage, lamplight, and flowers. It was the hour when Society, in slowly-parading carriages, would congregate to take the air beneath the pale mimosas that adorned the favourite promenade. All but recumbent, as though agreeably fatigued by their recent emotions, (what wild follies were not committed in shuttered-villas during the throbbing hours of noon?) the Cunans, in their elegant equipages, made for anyone, fresh from the provinces, an interesting and absorbing sight. The liquid-eyed loveliness of the women, and the handsomeness of the men, with their black moustaches and their treacherous smiles; these, indeed, were things to gaze on.

" Oh ki! " Miami laughed delightedly, indicating a foppish, pretty youth, holding in a restive little horse dancing away with him.

Rubbing herself repeatedly, as yet embarrassed by the novelty of her clothes, Edna could only gasp.

" . . . ," she jabbered, pointing at some flaunting belles in great evening hats and falling hair.

" All dat fine," Miami murmured, staring in wonderment around.

Dominating the city soared the Opera House, uplifting a big, naked man, all gilt, who was being bitten, or mauled, so it seemed, by a pack of wild animals carved of stone, while nearby were the University, and the Cathedral, with its low white dome crowned by moss-green tiles.

Making towards it, encouraged by the Vesper bell, some young girls, in muslin masks, followed by a retinue of bustling nuns, were running the gauntlet of the profligates that clustered on the curb.

" Oh, Jesus honey!" Edna cooed, scratching herself in an ecstasy of delight.

" Fo' shame, Chile, to act so unladylike; if any gen'leman look up he t'ink you make a wicked sign," Mrs. Mouth cautioned, stepping out upon the balcony from the sitting-room behind.

Inhaling a bottle of salvolatile, to dispel *de megrims,* she was looking dignified in a décolleté of smoke-blue tulle.

" Nebba do *dat* in s'ciety," she added, placing a protecting arm around each of her girls.

Seduced, not less than they, by the animation of the town, the fatigue of the journey seemed amply rewarded. It was amusing to watch the crowd before the Ciné Lara, across the way, where many were flocking attracted by the hectic posters of " A Wife's Revenge."

" I keep t'inking I see Nini Snagg," Mrs. Mouth observed, regarding a negress in emerald tinted silk, seated on a public-bench beneath the glittering greenery.

" Cunan folk dat fine," Edna twittered, turning about at her Father's voice:

> "W'en de day ob toil is done,
> W'en de race ob life is run,
> Heaven send thy weary one
> Rest for evermore! "

" Prancing nigger! Is it worth while to wear dose grimaces?"

" Sh'o, dis no good place to be."

" Why, what dair wrong wid it? "

" Ah set out to look fo' de Meetin'-House, but no sooner am Ah in de street, dan a female wid her har droopin' loose down ober her back, an' into her eyes, she tell me to Come along."

" Some of dose bold women, dey ought to be shot through dair bottoms! " Mrs. Mouth indignantly said.

" But I nebba answer nothin'."

" May our daughters respect dair virtue same as you! " Mrs. Mouth returned, focusing wistfully the vast flowery parterre of the Café McDhu'l.

Little city of cocktails, Cuna! The surpassing excellence of thy Barmen, who shall sing?

" See how dey spell ' Biar," Mammee,"
Miami tittered: " Dey forget de *i!* "
" Sh'o, chile, an' so dey do. . . ."
" Honey Jesus! " Edna broadly grinned:
" Imagine de ignorance ob dat."

VII

NOW, beyond the Alemeda, in the modish faubourg of Farananka, there lived a lady of both influence and wealth — the widow of the Inventor of Sunflower Piquant. Arbitress absolute of Cunan society, and owner, moreover, of a considerable portion of the town, the *veto* of Madame Ruiz, had caused the suicide indeed of more than one social climber. Unhappy, nostalgic, disdainful, selfish, ever about to abandon Cuna-Cuna to return to it no more, yet never budging, adoring her fairy villa far too well, Madame Ruiz while craving for the International-world, consoled herself by watching from afar European society going speedily to the dogs. Art loving, and considerably musical (many a dizzy venture at the Opera-house had owed its audition to her), she had, despite the self-centeredness of her nature, done not a little to render more brilliant the charming city it amused her with such vehemence to abuse.

One softly gloomy morning, preceding Madame Ruiz's first *cotillon* of the Season, the lodge-keeper of the Villa Alba, a negress, like some great, violet bug, was surprised, while tending the brightly-hanging Grape-Fruit in the drive, by an imperative knocking on the gate. At such a matutinal hour only trashy errand-boys shouldering baskets might be expected to call, and giving the summons no heed, the mulatress continued her work.

The Villa Alba, half-buried in spreading awnings, and surrounded by many noble trees, stood but a short distance off the mainroad, its pleasaunces enclosed by flower-enshrouded walls, all a-zig-zag, like the folds of a screen. Beloved of lizards, and velvet-backed humming-birds, the shaded gardens led on one side to the sea.

" To make such a noise at dis hour," the negress murmured, going grumblingly at length to the gate, disclosing upon opening, a gentleman in middle-life, with a toothbrush moustache and a sapphire ring.

" De mist'ess still in bed, sah."

" In bed ? "

" She out bery late sah, but you find Miss Edwards up."

And with a nod of thanks, the visitor directed his footsteps discreetly towards the house.

Although, not, precisely, *in* her bed when the caller, shortly afterwards, was announced, Madame Ruiz was nevertheless, as yet in *déshabille*.

" Tiresome man, what does he want to see me about? " she exclaimed, gathering around her a brocaded-wrap formed of a priestly cope.

" He referred to a lease, ma'am," the maid replied.

" A lease! " Madame Ruiz raised eyes dark with spleen.

The visit of her agent, or man of affairs, was apt to ruffle her composure for the day: " Tell him to leave it, and go," she commanded, selecting a nectarine from a basket of iced-fruits beside her.

Removing reflectively the sensitive skin, her mind evoked, in ironic review, the chief salient events of society, scheduled to take

place on the face of the map in the course
of the day.

The marriage of the Count de Nozhel, in
Touraine, to Mrs. Exelmans of Cincinnati,
the divorce of poor Lady Luckcock in
London (it seemed quite certain that one
of the five co-respondents was the little car-
rot-haired Lord Dubelly again), the last
"pomps," at Vienna, of Princess de
Seeyohl *née* Mitchening-Meyong (Peace to
her soul! She had led her life). . . . The
christening in Madrid of the girl-twins of
the Queen of Spain. . . .

"At her time, I really *don't* understand
it," Madame Ruiz murmured to herself
aloud, glancing, as though for an explanation, about the room.

Through the flowing folds of the mosquito
curtains of the bed, that swept a cool,
flagged-floor, spread with skins, shewed the
oratory, with its waxen flowers, and pendant
flickering lights, that burned, night and day,
before a Leonardo saint with a treacherous
smile. Beyond the little recess came a lacquer commode, bearing a masterly marble
group, depicting a pair of amorous herma-

phrodites amusing themselves, while above, against the spacious wainscoting of the wall, a painting of a man, elegantly corseted, with a Violet in his moustache, ' Study of a Parisian,' was suspended, and which, with its pendant ' Portrait of a Lady,' signed Van Dongen, were the chief outstanding objects that the room contained.

" One would have thought that at forty she would have given up having babies," Madame Ruiz mused, choosing a glossy cherry from the basket at her side.

Through the open window a sound of distant music caught her ear.

" Ah! If only he were less weak," she sighed, her thoughts turning towards the player, who seemed to be enamoured of the opening movement, (rapturously repeated), of *L'Après midi d'un Faune.*

The venetorial habits of Vittorio Ruiz, had been from his earliest years, the source of his mother's constant chagrin and despair. At the age of five he had assaulted his Nurse, and, steadily onward, his passions had grown and grown. . . .

" It's the fault of the wicked climate,"
Madame Ruiz reflected, as her companion,
Miss Edwards, came in with the post.

" Thanks, Eurydice," she murmured,
smilingly exchanging a butterfly kiss.

" It's going to be oh so hot, today! "

" Is it, dear? "

" Intense," Miss Edwards predicted,
fluttering a gay-daubed paper fan.

Sprite-like, with a little strained ghost-
face beneath a silver shock of hair, it
seemed as if her long blue eyes had absorbed
the Cunan sea.

" Do you remember the giant with the
beard? " she asked, " at the Presidency
fête? "

" Do I? "

" And we wondered who he could be! "

" Well? "

" He's the painter of Women's Backs,
my dear! "

" The painter of women's *what?* "

" An artist."

" Oh."

" I wanted to know if you'd advise me to
sit."

" Your back is charming, dear, *c'est un dos d'élite.*"

" I doubt, though, it's classic," Miss Edwards murmured, pirouetting slowly before the glass.

But Madame Ruiz was perusing her correspondence, and seemed to be absorbed.

" They're to be married, in Munich, on the fifth," she chirruped.

" Who? "

" Elsie and Baron Sitmar."

" Ah, Ta-ra, dear! In those far worlds. . . ." Miss Edwards impatiently exclaimed, opening wide a window and leaning out.

Beneath the flame-trees, with their spreading tops, one mass of crimson flower, cooly, white-garbed gardeners, with naked feet, and big bell-shaped hats of straw, were sweeping slowly, as in some rhythmic dance, the flamboyant blossoms that had fallen to the ground.

" Wasn't little Madame Haase, dear, born Kattie von Guggenheim? "

" I really don't know," Miss Edwards returned, flapping away a fly with her fan.

" This villanous climate! My memory's going. . . ."

"I wish I cared for Cuna less, that's all!" Miss Edwards said, her glance following a humming-bird, poised in air, above the sparkling turquoise of a fountain.

" Captain Moonlight . . . duty . . . (tedious word) . . . can't come! "

" Oh? "

" Such a dull post," Madame Ruiz murmured, pausing to listen to the persuasive tenor-voice of her son.

> " Little mauve nigger boy,
>   I t'ink you break my heart! "

" My poor Vitti! Bless him."

" He was out last night with some Chinese she."

" I understood him to be going to *Pelléas and Mélisande.*"

" He came to the Opera-house, but only for a minute."

" Dios! "

" And, oh, dearest," Miss Edwards dropped her cheek to her hand.

" Was Hatso as ever delicious? "

Madame Ruiz asked, changing the topic as her woman returned, followed by a pomeranian of parts, ' Snob '; a dog beautiful as a child.

" We had Gebhardt instead."

" In Mélisande she's so huge," Madame Ruiz commented, eyeing severely the legal-looking packet which her maid had brought her.

" Business, Camilla; *how* I pity you! " Madame Ruiz sighed.

" It seems," she said, " that for the next nine-and-ninety years, I have let a Villa to a Mr. and Mrs. Ahmadou Mouth."

VIII

FLOOR of copper, floor of gold. . . .
Beyond the custom-house door,
ajar, the street at sunrise seemed
aflame.

" Have you nothing, young man, to declare ? "

" . . . Butterflies ! "

" Exempt of duty. Pass."

Floor of silver, floor of pearl. . . .

Trailing a muslin net, and laughing for
happiness, Charlie Mouth marched into the
town.

Oh, Cuna-Cuna! Little city of Lies and
Peril! How many careless young nigger
boys have gone thus to seal their Doom?

Although the Sun-god was scarcely risen,
already the radiant street teemed with life.

Veiled dames, flirting fans, bent on
church or market, were issuing everywhere
from their doors, and the air was vibrant
with the sweet voice of bells.

To rejoin his parents promptly at their hotel, was a promise he was tempted to forget.

Along streets all fresh and blue in the shade of falling awnings, it was fine, indeed, to loiter. Beneath the portico of a church, a running fountain drew his steps aside. Too shy to strip and squat in the basin, he was glad to bathe freely his head, feet and chest: then stirred by curiosity to throw a glance at the building, he lifted the long yellow nets that veiled the door.

It was the fashionable church of La Favavoa, and the extemporary address of the Archbishop of Cuna was in full, and impassioned, swing.

" Imagine the world, my friends, had Christ been born a girl! " he was saying in tones of tender dismay as Charlie entered.

Subsiding bashfully to a bench, Charlie gazed around.

So many sparkling fans. One, a delicate light mauve one: " Shucks! If only you wa' butterflies! " he breathed, contemplating with avidity the nonchalant throng; then perceiving a richer specimen splashed

with silver of the same amative tint: " Oh
you lil beauty! " And, clutching his itch-
ing net to his heart, he regretfully withdrew.

Sauntering leisurely through the cool,
Mimosa-shaded streets, he approached, as
he guessed, the Presidency. A score of
shoeblacks, lolled at cards, or gossip, before
its gilded pales. Amazed at their audacity
(for the President had threatened more
than once to " wring the Public's neck "),
Charlie hastened by. Public gardens, brilliant with sarracenias, lay just beyond
the palace, where a music-pavilion, surrounded by palms and rocking-chairs, appeared a favourite, and much frequented
resort; from here he observed the Cunan
bay strewn with sloops and white-sailed
yachts, asleep upon the tide. Strolling on,
he found himself in the busy vicinity of the
Market. Although larger, and more varied,
it resembled, in other respects, the village
one at home.

" Say, honey, say " — crouching in the
dust before a little pyre of mangoes, a lean-
armed woman besought him to buy.

Pursued by a confusion of voices, he threaded his way deftly down an alley dressed with booths. Pomegranates, some open with their crimson seeds displayed, banana-combs, and big, veined watermelons, lay heaped on every side.

"I could do wid a slice ob watteh-million," he reflected: "but to lick an ice-cream, dat tempt me more!" Nor would the noble fruit of the baobab, the paw-paw, or the pine, turn him from his fancy.

But no ice-cream stand met his eye, and presently he resigned himself to sit down upon his heels, in the shade of a potter's stall, and consider the passing crowd.

Missionaries with freckled hands and hairy, care-worn faces, followed by pale girls wielding tambourines of the Army of the Soul, foppish nigger bucks in panamas and palm-beach suits so cocky, Chinamen with osier baskets, their nostalgic eyes aswoon, heavily straw-hatted nuns trailing their dust-coloured rags, and suddenly, oh could it be, but there was no mistaking that golden waddle: "Mamma!"

Mamma, Mammee, Mrs. Ahmadou Mouth.

All in white, with snow white shoes and hose so fine, he hardly dare.

" Mammee, Mammee, oh, Mammee . . . ."

" Sonny mine! My lil boy! "

" Mammee."

" Just to say! "

And, oh, honies! Close behind, behold Miami, and Edna too: The Miss Lips, the fair Lips, the smiling Lips. How spry each looked. The elder, (grown a trifle thinner), sweet *à ravir* in tomato-red, while her sister, plump as a cornfattened partridge, and very perceptibly powdered, seemed like the flower of the prairie sugar-cane when it breaks into bloom.

" We've been to a Music-hall, an' a pahty, an' Snowball has dropped black kittens." Forestalling Miami, Edna rapped it out.

" Oh, shucks! "

" An' since we go into s'ciety, we keep a boy in buttons! "

Mrs. Mouth turned about.

" Where is dat ijit coon? "

" He stay behind to bargain for de pee-wee birds Mammee, fo' to make de taht."

" De swindling tortoise."

" An' dair are no vacancies at de University: not fo' any ob us! " Edna further retailed going off into a spasm of giggles.

She was swinging a wicker basket, from which there dangled the silver forked tail of a fish.

" Fo' goodness sake gib dat sea-porcupine to Ibum, chile," Mrs. Mouth commanded, as a perspiring niggerling in livery presented himself.

" Ibum, his arms are full already."

" Just come along all to de Villa now? It dat mignon an' all so nice. An' after de collation," Mrs. Mouth (shocked on the servant's account at her son's nude neck), raised her voice: " we go to de habadasher in Palmbranch Avenue, an' I buy you an Eton colleh! "

IX

P RANCING Nigger, I t'ink it bery strange, dat Madame Ruiz, she nebba call."

" Sh'o."

" In August-Town, s'ciety less stuck-up dan heah! "

Ensconced in rocking-chairs, in the shade of the ample porch of the Villa Vista Hermosa, Mr. and Mrs. Mouth had been holding a desultory *tête-à-tête*.

It was a Sabbath evening, and a sound of reedy pipes and bafalons, from a neighbouring café, filled with a feverish sadness the brilliantly lamp-lit street.

" De airs ob de nabehs, dat dair affair, what matter mo', am de chillens schoolin'."

" Prancing Nigger, I hope your Son an' Daughters will yet take dair Degrees, an' if not from de University, den from Home. From heah."

" Hey-ho-day, an' dat would be a miracle! " Mr. Mouth mirthlessly laughed.

287

" Dose chillens hab learnt quite a lot already."

" 'Bout de shaps an' cynemas! "

Mrs. Mouth disdained a reply.

She had taken the girls to the gallery at the Opera one night to hear ' Louise,' but they had come out, by tacit agreement, in the middle of it: the plainness of Louise's blouse, and the lack of tunes . . . added to which, the suffocation of the gallery . . . And — once bit twice shy — they had not gone back again.

" All your fambly need, Prancing Nigger, is social opportunity! But what is de good ob de Babtist parson? "

Mr. Mouth sketched a gesture.

" Sh'o, Edna, she some young yet. . . . But Miami dat distinguée; an', doh I her mother, b'lieb me dat is one ob de choicest girls I see; an' dat's de trute."

" It queer," Mr. Mouth abstrusely murmured, " how many skeeter-bugs dair are 'bout dis ebenin'! "

" De begonias in de window-boxes most lik'ly draw dem. But as I was saying Prancing Nigger, I t'ink it bery strange dat Madame Ruiz nebba call."

" P'raps, she out ob town."

" Accordin' to de paper, she bin habing her back painted, but what dat fo' I dunno."

" Ah shouldn't wonder ef she hab some trouble ob a dorsal kind; same as me gramma mumma long agone."

" Dair'd be no harm in sendin' one ob de chillens to enquire. Wha' you t'ink, sah?" Mrs. Mouth demanded, plucking from off the porch a pale hanging flower with a languorous scent.

Mr. Mouth glanced apprehensively skyward.

The mutters of thunder and intermittent lightning of the finest nights.

" It's a misfortnit we eber left Mediavilla," he exclaimed uneasily, as a falling star, known as a thief star, sped swiftly down the sky.

" Prancing Nigger," Mrs. Mouth rose remarking, " befo' you start to grummle, I leab you alone to your Jereymiads! "

" A misfortnit sho' nuff," he mused, and regret for the savannah country, and the tall palm trees of his village, oppressed his heart. Moreover, his means (derived from the cultivation of the *Musa paradisica,* or Banana), seemed likely to prove ere long inadequate to support the whims of his wife, who after a lifetime of contented nudity, appeared to be now almost insatiable for dress.

A discordant noise from above interrupted the trend of his thoughts.

" Sh'o, she plays wid it like a toy," he sighed, as the sound occurred again.

" Prancing Nigger, de water-supply cut off! "

" It's de Lord's will."

" Dair's not a drop my lub in de privy."

" 'Cos it always in use! "

" I b'lieb dat lil half-caste Ibum, 'cos I threaten to gib him notice, do somet'in' out ob malace to de chain."

" Whom de Lord Loveth, He chasteneth! " Mr. Mouth observed, " an' dose bery words (ef you look) you will find in de twelfth chapter, an' de sixth berse ob de Book ob Hebrews."

" Prancing Nigger, you datways selfish! Always t'inkin' ob your soul, instead ob your obligations towards de fambly."

" Why, wha' mo' can I do dan I've done ? "

Mrs. Mouth faintly shrugged.

" I had hoped," she said, " dat Nini would hab bin ob use to de girls, but dat seem now impossible! " For Mrs. Snagg had been traced to a house of ill-fame, where, it appeared, she was an exponent of the Hodeidah — a lascive Cunan dance.

" Understand dat any sort ob intimacy 'tween de Villa an' de *Closerie des Lilas* Ah must flatly forbid."

" Prancing Nigger, as ef I should take your innocent chillens to call on po' Nini; not dat eberyt'ing about her at de *Closerie* is not elegant an' nice. Sh'o, some ob de inmates ob dat establishment possess mo' diamonds dan dair betters do outside! You'd be surprised ef you could see what two ob de girls dair, Dinah an' Lew. . . ."

" Enuf! "

" It isn't always Virtue, Prancing Nigger, dat come off best! " And Mrs. Mouth might have offered further observations on the matter of ethics, had not her husband left her.

X

PAST the Presidency and the public park, the Theatres Maxine Bush, Eden-Garden, and Apollo, along the Avenida, and the Jazz-halls by the wharf, past little suburban shops, and old, deserted churchyards where bloom geraniums, through streets of squalid houses, and onward skirting pleasure lawns and orchards, bibbitty-bobbitty, beneath the sovereign brightness of the sky, the Farananka tram crawled along.

Surveying the landscape listlessly through the sticks of her fan, Miss Edna Mouth grew slightly bored — alas, poor child; couldst thou have guessed the blazing brightness of thy Star, thou wouldst doubtless have been more alert!

" Sh'o, it dat far an' tejus," she observed to the conductor, lifting upon him the sharp-soft eyes of a parroquet.

She was looking bewitching in a frock of silverish *mousseleine* and a violet tallyho cap, and dangled upon her knees an intoxicating sheaf of blossoms, known as Marvel of Peru.

"Hab patience lil Missey, an' we soon be dah."

*   *   *   *   *   *

"He tells me, dear child, he tells me," Madame Ruiz was rounding a garden path, upon the arm of her son, "he tells me, Vitti, that the systole and diastole of my heart's muscles are slightly inflamed; and, that, I ought, darling, to be *very* careful. . . ."

Followed by a handsome borzoi, and the pomeranian Snob, the pair were taking their usual post-prandial exercise beneath the trees.

"Let me come, mother, dear," he murmured without interrupting, "over the other side of you; I always like to be on the right side of my profile!"

"And, really, since the affair of Madame de Bazvalon, my health has hardly been what it was."

"That foolish little woman," he uncomfortably laughed.

"He tells me my nerves need rest," she

declared, looking pathetically up at him.

He had the nose of an actress, and ink-black hair streaked with gold, his eyes seemed to be covered with the freshest of fresh dark pollen, while nothing could exceed the vivid pallor of his cheeks, or the bright sanguine of his mouth.

" You go out so much, Mother."

" Not so much! "

" So very much."

" And he forbids me my opera-box for the rest of the week! So last night I sat at home dear child reading the Life of Lazarillo de Tormes."

" I don't give a damn," he said, " for any of your doctors."

" So vexing though; and apparently Lady Bird has been at death's door, and poor Peggy Povey too. It seems she got wet on the way to the Races: and really I was *sorry* for her when I saw her in the paddock; for the oats and the corn, and the wheat and the tares, and the barley and the rye, and all the rest of the reeds and grasses in her pretty Lancret hat, looked like nothing so much as manure."

" I adore to folly her schoolboy's moustache! "

" My dear, Age is the one disaster," Madame Ruiz remarked, raising the rosy dome of her sunshade a degree higher above her head.

They were pacing a walk radiant with trees and flowers as some magician's garden, that commanded a sweeping prospect of long, livid sands, against a white green sea.

" There would seem to be several new yachts, darling," Madame Ruiz observed.

" The duke of Wellclose with his duchess (on their wedding-tour) arrived with the tide."

" Poor man; I'm told that he only drove to the church after thirty brandies! "

" And the Sea-Thistle, with Lady Violet Valesbridge, and, *oh*, such a crowd."

" She used to be known as ' The Cat of Curzon Street,' but I hear she is still quite amazingly pretty," Madame Ruiz murmured, turning to admire a somnolent peacock, with moping fan, poised upon the curved still arm of a marble mænad.

" How sweet something smells."

" It's the China lilies."

" I believe it's my handkerchief . . ."
he said.

" Vain wicked boy; ah, if you would but
decide, and marry some nice, intelligent
girl."

" I'm too young yet."

" You're *twenty-six!* "

" And past the age of folly-o," he made
airy answer, drawing from his breast-
pocket a flat, jewel-encrusted case, and
lighting a cigarette.

" Think of the many men, darling, of
twenty-six . . ." Madame Ruiz broke off,
focussing the fruit-bearing summit of a
slender arecia palm.

" Foll-foll-folly-o!" he laughed.

" I think I'm going in."

" Oh, why? "

" Because," Madame Ruiz repressed a
yawn, " because, dear, I feel armchairish."

With a kiss of the finger tips (decidedly
distinguished hands had Vittorio Ruiz), he
turned away.

Joying frankly in excess, the fiery noontide hour had a special charm for him.

It was the hour, to be sure, of " the Fawn! "

" Aho, Ahi, Aha! " he carolled, descending half-trippingly a few white winding stairs, that brought him upon a fountain. Palms, with their floating fronds, radiating light, stood all around.

It was here " the creative mood " would sometimes take him, for he possessed no small measure of talent of his own.

His *Three Hodeidahs,* and *Five Phallic Dances for Pianoforte and Orchestra,* otherwise known as " Suite in Green," had taken the whole concert world by storm, and, now, growing more audacious, he was engaged upon an opera to be known, by and by, as *Sumaïa.*

" Ah Atthis, it was Sappho who told me — " tentatively he sought an air.

A touch of banter there.

" *Ah Atthis* — " One must make the girl feel that her little secret is out . . . ; quiz her; but let her know, and pretty plain, that the Poetess had been talking. . . .

" Ah Atthis — "

But somehow or other the lyric mood

today was obdurate, and not to be per-
suaded.

" I blame the oysters! After oysters — "
he murmured, turning about to ascertain
what was exciting the dogs.

She was coming up the drive with her
face to the sun, her body shielded behind a
spreading bouquet of circumstance.

" It's all right; they'll not hurt you."

" Sh'o, I not afraid! "

" Tell me who it is you wish to see."

" Mammee send me wid dese flowehs. . . ."

" Oh! But how scrumptious."

" It strange how dey call de bees; honey-
bees, sweat-bees, bumble-bees an' all! " she
murmured, shaking the blossoms into the
air.

" That's only natural," he returned, his
hand falling lightly to her arm.

" Madame Ruiz is in? "

" She is: but she is resting; and something tells me," he suavely added, indicating a grassy bank, " you might care to re-
pose yourself too."

And indeed after such a long and rambling course, she was glad to accept.

" De groung's as soft as a cushom," she purred, sinking with nonchalance to the grass.

" You'd find it," he said, " even softer, if you'll try it nearer me."

" Dis a mighty pretty place! "

" And you — " but he checked his tongue.

" Fo' a villa so grand, dair must be mo' dan one privy? "

" Some six, or seven! "

" Ours is broke."

" You should get it mended."

" De aggervatines'! " she wriggled.

" Tell me about them."

And so, not without digressions, she unfolded her life.

" Then you, Charlie, and Mimi are here, dear, to study? "

" As soon as de University is able to receibe us; but dair's a waiting-list already dat long."

" And what do you do with all your spare time? "

" Goin' round de shops takes up some ob

it. An' den ob course, dair's de Cinés. Oh,
I love de Lara. We went last night to see
Souls in Hell."

" I've not been! "

" Oh it was choice."

" Was it? Why? "

" De scene ob dat story," she told him,
" happen foreign; 'way crost de big watteh,
on de odder side ob de world . . . an' de
principal gal, she merried to a man who
neglect her (ebery ebenin' he go to pahtys
an' biars) while all de time his wife she
sit at home wid her lil pickney at her breas'.
But dair anodder gemplum (a friend ob de
fambly) an' he afiah to woe her; but she
only shake de head, slowly, from side to
side, an' send dat man away. Den de hub-
som lose his fortune, an', oh, she dat
'stracted, she dat crazed . . . at last, she
take to gamblin', but dat only make t'ings
worse. Den de friend ob de fambly come
back, an' offer to pay all de expenses ef
only she unbend: so she cry, an' she cry,
'cos it grieb her to leab her pickney to de
neglect ob de serbants (dair was three ob
dem, an old buckler, a boy, an' a cook) but,

PRANCING NIGGER

in de end, she do, an' frtt! away she go in de fambly carriage. An' den, bimeby, you see dem in de bedroom doin' a bit ob funning."

"What?"

"Oh ki; it put me in de gigglemints...."

"Exquisite kid."

"Sh'o, de coffee-concerts an' de pictchures, I don't nebba tiah ob dem."

"Bad baby."

"I turned thirteen."

"You are?"

"By de Law ob de Island, I a spinster ob age!"

"I might have guessed it was the Bar! These Law-students," he murmured, addressing the birds.

"Sh'o, it's de trute," she pouted, with a languishing glance through the sticks of her fan.

"I don't doubt it," he answered, taking lightly her hand.

"Mercy," she marvelled: "is dat a watch dah, on your arm?"

"Dark, bright baby!"

"Oh, an' de lil 'V.R.' all in precious

302

stones so blue," her frail fingers caressed his wrist.

"Exquisite kid." She was in his arms.

"Vitti, Vitti! — " It was the voice of Eurydice Edwards. Her face was strained and quivering. She seemed about to faint.

XI

EVER so lovely are the young men of Cuna-Cuna — Juarez, Jotifa, Enid — (these, from many, to distinguish but a few) — but none so delicate, charming, and squeamish, as Charlie Mouth.

" Attractive little Rose. . . ." " What a devil of a dream . . ." the avid belles would exclaim when he walked abroad, while impassioned widows would whisper " Peach! "

One evening, towards sundown, just as the city lifts its awnings, and the deserted streets start seething with delight, he left his home to enjoy the grateful air. It had been a day of singular oppressiveness, and not expecting overmuch of the vesperal breezes, he had borrowed his mother's small Pompadour fan.

Ah, little did that nigger boy know as he strolled along what novel emotions that promenade held in store!

Disrelishing the dust of the Avenida, he directed his steps towards the Park.

He had formed already an acquaintance-ship with several young men, members, it seemed, of the University, and these he would sometimes join, about this hour, beneath the Calabash-trees in the Marcella Gardens.

There was Abe, a lad of fifteen, whose father ran a Jazz Hall on the harbour-beach, and Ramon, who was destined to enter the Church, and the intriguing Esmé, whose dream was the Stage, and who was supposed to be " in touch " with Miss Maxine Bush, and there was Pedro, Pedro ardent and obese, who seemed to imagine that to be a dress-designer to foreign Princesses would yield his several talents a thrice-blessed harvest.

Brooding on these and other matters, Charlie found himself in Liberty Square.

Here, the Cunan Poet, Samba Marcella's effigy arose — that " sable singer of Revolt."

Aloft, on a pedestal, soared the Poet, laurel-crowned, thick-lipped, woolly, a large weeping Genius, with a bold taste for draperies, hovering just beneath; her one eye closed, the other open, giving her an air of winking confidentially at the passers-by: " Up Cunans, up! To arms, to arms! " he quoted, lingering to watch the playful swallows wheeling among the tubs of roseoleanders that stood around.

And a thirst, less for bloodshed, than for a sherbet, seized him.

It was a square noted for the frequency of its bars, and many of their names, in flickering lights, shewed palely forth already.

Cuna! City of Moonstones; how faeric art thou in the blue blur of dusk!

Costa Rica. Chile Bar. To the Island of June. . . .

Red roses, against tall mirrors, reflecting the falling night.

Seated before a cloudy cocktail, a girl with gold cheeks like the flesh of peaches, addressed him softly from behind: " Listen, lion! "

But he merely smiled on himself in the

polished mirrors, displaying moist-gleaming teeth and coral gums.

An aroma of aromatic cloves . . . a mystic murmur of ice. . . .

A little dazed after a Ron Bacardi, he moved away: " Shine sah? " the inveigling squeak of a shoeblack followed him.

Sauntering by the dusty benches by the pavement-side, where white-robed negresses sat communing in twos and threes, he attained the Avenue Messalina with its spreading palms, whose fronds hung nerveless in the windless air.

Tinkling mandolines from restaurant gardens, light laughter, and shifting lights.

Passing before the Café de Cuna, and a people's " Dancing," he roamed leisurely along. Incipient Cyprians, led by vigilant, blanched-faced queens, youths of a certain life, known as bwam-wams, gaunt pariah-dogs with questing eyes, all equally were on the prowl. Beneath the Pharaohic pilasters of the Theatre Maxine Bush, a street crowd had formed before a notice described " Important," which informed the Public, that owing to a " temporary hoarseness," the rôle of Miss Maxine Bush would be taken, on that occasion, by Miss Pauline Collier.

The Marcella Gardens lay towards the end of the Avenue, in the animated vicinity of the Opera. Pursuing the glittering thoroughfare, it was interesting to observe the pleasure announcements of the various theatres, picked out in signs of fire: *Aïda: The Jewels of the Madonna: Marthe Regnier's Season.*

Vending bags of roasted peanuts, or sapadillos and avocado pears, insistent small boys were importuning the throng.

" Go away; I can't be bodder," Charlie was saying, when he seemed to slip; it was as though the pavement were a carpet snatched from under him, and looking round, he was surprised to see, in a Confectioner's window, a couple of marble-topped tables start merrily waltzing together.

Driven onward by those behind, he began stumblingly to run towards the Park. It was the general goal. Footing it a little ahead, two loose women and a gay young man (pursued by a waiter with a napkin and a bill), together with the horrified, half-crazed crowd; all, helter-skelter, were intent upon the Park.

Above the Calabash trees, bronze, demoniac, the moon gleamed sourly from a starless sky, and although not a breath of air was stirring, the crests of the loftiest palms were set arustling by the vibration at their roots.

" Oh, will nobody *stop* it?" a terror-struck lady implored.

Feeling quite white and clasping a fetish, Charlie sank all panting to the ground.

Safe from falling chimney-pots and sign-boards, that, for " Pure Vaseline," for instance, had all but caught him, he had much to be thankful for.

" Sh'o nuff, dat was a close shave," he gasped, gazing dazed about him.

Clustered back to back nearby upon the grass, three stolid matrons, matrons of hoary England, evidently not without previous earthquake experience, were ignoring resolutely the repeated shocks:

" I always follow the Fashions, dear, at a distance!" one was saying: " this little

gingham gown I'm wearing, I had made for
me after a design I found in a newspaper
at my hotel."

"It must have been a pretty old one,
dear — I mean the paper, of course."

"New things are only those you know
that have been forgotten."

"Mary . . . there's a sharp pin, sweet,
at the back of your . . . *Oh!*"

Venturing upon his legs, Charlie turned
away.

By the Park palings a few "Salvation-
ists" were holding forth, while in the
sweep before the bandstand, the artists
from the Opera in their costumes of Aïda,
were causing almost a greater panic, among
the ignorant, than the earthquake was itself. A crowd promiscuous rather than
representative, composed variously of
chauffeurs (making a wretched pretence,
poor chaps, of seeking out their masters),
Cyprians, patricians (these in opera cloaks
and sparkling diamonds), tourists. for
whom the Hodeidah girls would *not* dance
that night, and bwam-wam bwam-wams,
whose equivocal behaviour, indeed, was per-

haps more shocking even than the shocks, set the pent Park ahum. Yet, notwithstanding the upheavals of Nature, certain persons there were bravely making new plans.

" How I wish I could, dear! But I shall be having a houseful of women over Sunday — that's to say."

" Then come the week after."

" Thanks, then, I *will*."

Hoping to meet with Abe, Charlie took a pathway, flanked with rows of tangled roses, whose leaves shook down at every step.

And it occurred to him with alarming force that perhaps he was an orphan.

Papee, Mammee, Mimi and lil Edna — the villa drawing-room on the floor. . . .

His heart stopped still.

" An' dey in de spirrit world — in heaven hereafter! " He glanced with awe at the moon's dark disk.

" All in dair cotton shrouds . . ."

What if he should die and go to the Bad Place below?

" I mizzable sinneh Lord. You heah

Sah? You heah me say dat? Oh, Jesus, Jesus, Jesus," and weeping, he threw himself down among a bed of flowers.

When he raised his face it was towards a sky all primrose and silver pink. Sunk deep in his dew laved bower, it was sweet to behold the light. Above him great spikes of blossom were stirring in the idle wind, while birds were piping anthems among the palms. And in thanksgiving, too, arose the matins bells. From Our Lady of the Pillar, from the church of La Favavoa in the West, from Saint Sebastian, from Our Lady of the Sea, from Our Lady of Mount Carmel, from Santa Theresa, from Saint Francis of the Poor.

XII

B UT although by the grace of Providence, the city of Cuna-Cuna had
been spared, other parts of the island
had sustained irremediable loss. In the
Province of Casuby, beyond the May Day
Mountains, many a fair Banana, or Sugar
estate, had been pitifully wrecked, yet what
caused perhaps the widest regret among the
Cunan public, was the destruction of the
famous convent of Sasabonsam. One of the
beauties of the island, one of the gems of
tropic architecture celebrated, made immortal (in *The Picnic*), by the Poet Marcella, had disappeared. A Relief Fund for
those afflicted had at once been started, and
as if this were not enough, the doors of the
Villa Alba were about to be thrown open for
" An Evening of Song and Gala," in the
causes of charity.

" Prancing Nigger, dis an event to take
exvantage ob; dis not a lil t'ing love to be
sneezed at at all," Mrs. Mouth eagerly said

upon hearing the news, and she had gone about ever since, reciting the names of the list of Patronesses, including that of the Cunan Archbishop.

It was the auspicious evening.

In their commodious, jointly-shared bedroom, the Miss Lips, the fair Lips, the smiling Lips were maiding one another in what they both considered to be the " Parisian way "; a way, it appeared, that involved much nudging, arch laughter, and, even, some prodding.

" In love? Up to my ankles! Oh, yes." Edna blithely chuckled.

" Up to your topnot! " her sister returned, making as if to pull it.

But with the butt end of the curlingtongs, Edna waved her away.

Since her visit to the Villa Alba " me, an' Misteh Ruiz " was all her talk, and to be his reigning mistress the summit of her dreams.

" Come on man wid dose tongs; 'cos I want 'em myself," Miami murmured, pinning a knot of the sweet Night Jasmyn deftly above her ear.

Its aroma evoked Bamboo.

Oh, why had he not joined her? Why did he delay? Had he forgotten their delight among the trees, the giant silk cotton trees, with the hammer-tree-frogs chanting in the dark: Rig-a-jig-jig, rig-a-jig-jig?

" Which you like de best man, dis lil necklash or de odder? " Edna asked, essaying a strand of orchid tinted beads about her throat.

" I'd wear dem both," her sister advised.

" I t'ink, on de whole, I wear de odder; de one he gib me de time he take exvantage ob my innocence."

" Since dose imitation pearls, honey, — he gib you anyt'ing else? "

" No; but he dat generous! He say he mean to make me a lil pickney gal darter: An', oh, won't dat be a day," Edna fluted, breaking off at the sound of her mother's voice in the corridor.

" . . . and tell de cabman to take de fly-bonnets off de horses," she was instructing Ibum as she entered the room.

She had a gown of the new mignonette

satin, with " episcopal " sleeves lined with red.

" Come girls, de cab is waiting; but perhaps you no savey dat."

They didn't; and, for some time, dire was the confusion.

In the Peacock drawing-room of the Villa Alba, the stirring ballet music from *Isfahan,* filled the vast room with its thrilling madness. Upon a raised estrade, a corps of dancing boys from Sankor, had glided amid a murmur of applause.

The combination of charity and amusement had brought together a crowded, and cosmopolitan assembly, and early though it was it was evident already, that with many more new advents there would be a shortage of chairs. From their yachts had come several distinguished birds of passage, exhaling an atmosphere of Paris and Park Lane.

Wielding a heavy bouquet of black feathers, Madame Ruiz, robed in a gown of malmaison cloth-of-silver, watched the dancers from an alcove by the door.

Their swaying torsos, and weaving gliding feet, fettered with chains of orchids and hung with bells, held a fascination for her.

" My dear they beat the Hodeidahs! I'm sure I never saw anything like it," the Duchess of Wellclose remarked admiringly: " That little one Fred," she murmured, turning towards the Duke.

A piece of praise, a staid, small body in a demure lace cap chanced to hear.

This was " the incomparable " Miss McAdam, the veteran ballet mistress of the Opera-house, and inventrix of the dance. Born in the frigid High Street of Aberdeen, " Alice," as she was universally known among enthusiastic patrons of the ballet, had come originally to the tropics as companion to a widowed clergyman in Orders, when, as she would relate (in her picturesque, native brogue), at the sight of *Nature* her soul had awoke. Self-expression had come with a rush; and, now, that she was ballet mistress of the Cunan opera, some of the daring *ensembles* of the Scottish spinster, would embarrass, even the good Cunans themselves.

" I've warned the lads," she whispered to

Madame Ruiz: " to cut their final figure, on account of the Archbishop. But young boys (bless their little —) are so excitable, and I expect that they'll forget! "

Gazing on their perfect backs, Madame Ruiz could not but mourn the fate of the Painter, who, like Dalow, had specialized almost exclusively, on this aspect of the human form; for, alas, that admirable Artist had been claimed by the Quake; and although his portrait of Madame Ruiz remained unfinished . . . there was still a mole, nevertheless, in gratitude, and as a mark of respect, she had sent her Rolls car to the Mass in honour of his obsequies, with the *crêpe* off an old black dinner-dress tied across the lamps.

" I see they're going to," Miss McAdam murmured, craning a little to focus the Archbishop, then descanting to two ladies with deep purple fans.

" Ah, well! It's what they do in *Isfahan,*" Madame Ruiz commented, turning to greet her neighbour Lady Bird.

" Am I late for Gebhardt ? " she asked, as if Life itself hinged upon the reply.

A quietly silly woman, Madame Ruiz was often obliged to lament the absence of intellect at her door: accounting for it as the consequence of a weakness for negroes, combined with a hopeless passion for the Regius Professor of Greek at Oxford.

But the strident cries of the dancers, and the increasing volume of the music, discouraged all talk, though ladies with collection-boxes (biding their time) were beginning furtively to select their next quarry.

Countess Katty Taosay, *née* Soderini, a little woman and sure of the giants, could feel in her psychic veins which men were most likely to empty their pockets: English Consul . . . pale and interesting, he not refuse to stoop and fumble, nor Follinsbe 'Peter,' the slender husband of a fashionable wife, or Charlie Campfire, a young boy like an injured camel, heir to vast banana estates, the darling, and six foot high if an inch.

" Why do big men like little women? " she wondered, waving a fan powdered with blue *paillettes:* and she was still casting about for a reason, when the hectic music stopped.

And now the room echoed briefly with applause, while admiration was divided between the superexcellence of the dancers, and the living beauty of the rugs which their feet had trod — rare rugs from Bokhara-i-Shareef, and Kairouan-city-of-Prayer, lent by the mistress of the house.

Entering on the last hand-clap, Mr. and Mrs. Mouth, followed by their daughters, felt, each, in their several ways, they might expect to enjoy themselves.

" Prancing Nigger, what a *furore!* " Mrs. Mouth exclaimed. " You b'lieb, I hope, now, dat our tickets was worth de money."

Plucking at the swallow-tails of an evening ' West-End,' Mr. Mouth was disinclined to reopen a threadbare topic.

" It queah how few neegah dair be," he observed, scanning the brilliant audience, many of whom, taking advantage of an interval, were flocking towards a buffet in an adjoining conservatory.

" Prancing Nigger, I feel I could do wid a glass ob champagne."

Passing across a corridor, it would have been interesting to have explored the spacious vistas that loomed beyond: " Dat must be one ob de priveys," Edna murmured, pointing to a distant door.

" Seben, chile, did you say? "

" If not more! "

" She seem fond ob flowehs," Mr. Mouth commented, pausing to notice the various plants that lined the way: from the roof swung showery azure flowers that commingled with the theatrically-hued cañas, set out in crude, bold, colour-schemes below, that looked best at night. But in their malignant splendour, the orchids were the thing. Mrs. Abanathy, Ronald Firbank, (a dingy lilac blossom of rarity untold), Prince Palairet, a heavy blue-spotted flower, and rosy Olive Moonlight, were those that claimed the greatest respect from a few discerning connoisseurs.

" Prancing Nigger, you got a chalk mark on your ' West-End,' come heah, sah, an' let me brush it."

Hopeful of glimpsing Vittorio, Miami and Edna sauntered on. With arms loosely entwined about each other's hips, they made in their complete insouciance, a conspicuous couple.

" I'd give sumpin' to see de bedrooms, man, 'cos dair are chapels, and' barf-rooms, besides odder conveniences off dem," Edna related, returning a virulent glance from Miss Eurydice Edwards, with a contemptuous, pitying smile.

Traversing a throng, sampling sorbets, and ices, the sisters strolled out upon the lawn.

The big silver stars how clear they shone — infinitudes, infinitudes. . . .

" Adieu, hydrangeas, adieu, blue, burning South! "

The concert, it seemed, had begun.

" Come chillens, come! "

In the vast drawing-room, the first novelty of the evening — an aria from *Sumaïa* — had stilled all chatter. Deep-sweet, poignant, the singer's voice was conjuring Sumaïa's farewell to the Greek isle of Mitylene, bidding farewell to its gracious women, and to the trees of white, or turquoise, in the gardens of Lesbos.

" Adieu, hydrangeas — "

Hardly a suitable moment, perhaps, to dispute a chair! But neither the duchess of Wellclose or Mrs. Mouth were creatures easily abashed.

" I pay, an' I mean to hab it."

" You can't; it's taken! " the duchess returned, nodding meaningly towards the buffet, where the duke could be seen swizzling whiskey at the back of the bar.

" Sh'o! Dese white women seem to t'ink dey can hab ebberyt'ing."

" Taken," the duchess repeated, who disliked what she called the *parfum d'Afrique* of the " sooties," and as though to intimidate Mrs. Mouth, she gave her a look that would have made many a Peeress in London quail.

Nevertheless in the stir that followed the song, chairs were forthcoming.

" From de complexion dat female hab, she look as doh she bin boiling bananas! " Mrs. Mouth commented comfortably, loud enough for the duchess to hear.

" Such a large congregation should su'tinly assist de fund! " Mr. Mouth re-

sourcefully said, envisaging with interest
the audience; it was not every day that one
could feast the gaze on the noble baldness
of the Archbishop, or on the subtle *silhouette* of Miss Maxine Bush, swathed like
an idol in an Egyptian tissue woven with
magical eyes.

"De woman in de window dah," Mrs.
Mouth remarked, indicating a dowager who
had the hard, but resigned look of the
Mother of six daughters, in immediate succession, "hab a look, Prancing Nigger, ob
your favourite statesman."

"De immortal Wilberforce!"

"I s'poge it's de whiskers," Mrs. Mouth
replied, ruffling gently her "Borgia"
sleeves for the benefit of the Archbishop.
Rumour had it he was fond of negresses,
and that the black private secretary he employed was his own natural son, while some
suspected indeed a less natural connexion.

But Madame Hatso (of Blue Brazil, the
Argentine; those nights in Venezuela and
Buenos Ayres, "bis" and "bravas"!
How the public had roared) was curtseying
right and left, and glancing round to address

her daughters, Mrs. Mouth perceived with vexation that Edna had vanished.

In the garden he caught her to him:
" Flower of the Sugar cane!"
" Misteh Ruiz. . . ."
" Exquisite kid."
" I saw you thu de window-glass all de time, an' dair was I! laughing so silent-ly. . . ."
" My little honey."
" . . . no; 'cos ob de nabehs," she fluted, drawing him beneath the great flamboyants that stood like temples of darkness all around.
" Sweetheart."
" I 'clar to grashis!" she delightedly crooned as he gathered her up in his arms.
" My little Edna. . . . ? . . . ? . . . ?"
" Where you goin' wid me to?"
" There," and he nodded towards the white sea sand.

A yawning butler, an insolent footman, a snoring coachman, a drooping horse. . . .
The last conveyance had driven away, and

only a party of " b — d — y niggers," supposed to be waiting for their daughter, was keeping the domestics from their bed.

Ernest, the bepowdered footman, believed them to be thieves, and could have sworn he saw a tablespoon in the old coon's pocket.

Hardly able to restrain his tears, Mr. Mouth sat gazing vacuously at the floor.

" Wha' can keep de chile? . . . Oh Lord . . . I hope dair noddin' wrong."

" On such a lovely ebenin' what is time! " Mrs. Mouth exclaimed, taking up an attitude of night-enchantment by the open door.

A remark that caused Butler, and subordinate, to cough.

" It not often I see de cosmos look so special! "

" Ef she not heah soon, we better go widout her," Miami murmured, who was examining the visitors cards on the hall table undismayed by the eye of Ernest.

It's odd she should so procrastinate; but la jeunesse, c'est le temps ou l'on s'amuse," Mrs. Mouth blandly declared, seating herself tranquilly by her husband's side.

" Dair noddin', I hope, de matteh. . . ."

" Eh, suz, my deah! Eh, suz." Reassuringly, she tapped his arm.

" Sir Victor Virtue, Lady Bird, Princess Altamisal, " Miami tossed their cards.

" Sh'o it was a charming ebenin' ! Doh I was sorry for de duchess, wid de duke, an' he all nasty drunk wid spirits."

" I s'poge she use to it."

" It was a perfect skangle! Howebber, on de whole, it was quite an enjoyable pahty — doh dat music ob Wagner, it gib me de retches."

" It bore me, too," Miami confessed, as a couple of underfootmen made their appearance, and joining their fidgeting colleagues by the door, waited for the last guests to depart, in a mocking, whispering group.

" Ef she not here bery soon," Miami murmured, vexed by the servants impertinent smiles.

" Sh'o, she be here directly," Mrs. Mouth returned, appraising through her fan-sticks the footman's calves.

" It daybreak already! " Miami yawned,

329

moved to elfish mirth by the overemphasis
of rouge on her mother's round cheeks.

But under the domestics' mocking stare,
their talk at length was chilled to silence.

From the garden came the plaintive
wheepling of a bird, (intermingled with the
coachman's spasmodic snores), while above
the awning of the door, the stars were wanly
paling.

" Prancing nigger, sah, heah de day.
Dair no good waitin' any more."

It was on their return from the Villa
Alba, that they found a letter signed
' Mamma Luna,' announcing the death of
Bamboo.

XIII

H E HAD gone out it seemed upon the sea to avoid the earthquake (leaving his mother at home to take care of the shop), but the boat had overturned, and the evil sharks . . .

In a room darkened against the sun, Miami, distracted, wept. Crunched by the maw of a great blue shark: " Oh honey."

Face downward with one limp arm dangling to the floor, she bemoaned her loss: such love-blank, and aching void! Like some desolate, empty cave, filled with clouds, so her heart.

" An' to t'ink dat I eber teased you! " she moaned, reproaching herself for the heedless past; and as day passed over day, still she wept.

One mid-afternoon, it was some two weeks later, she was reclining lifelessly across the bed, gazing at the sunblots on the floor. There had been a mild disturbance of a volcanic nature that morning, and indeed slight though unmistakable shocks, had been sensed repeatedly of late.

" Intercession " services, fully choral — the latest craze of society — filled the churches at present, sadly at the expense of other places of amusement; many of which had been obliged to close down. A religious revival was in the air, and in the Parks and streets elegant dames would stop one another in their passing carriages, and pour out the stories of their iniquitous lives.

Disturbed by the tolling of a neighbouring bell, Miami reluctantly rose.

" Lord! What a din; it gib a po' soul de grabe-yahd creeps," she murmured, lifting the jalousie of a sun-shutter and peering idly out.

Standing in the street was a Chinese Laundrymaid, chatting with two Chinamen with osier baskets, while a gaunt pariah dog was rummaging among some egg-shells and banana-skins in the dust before the gate.

" Dat lil fool-fool Ibum, he throw ebberyt'ing out ob de window, an' nebba t'ink ob de stink," she commented, as an odour of decay was wafted in on a gust of the hot trade wind. The trade winds! How pleasantly they used to blow in the village of Mediavilla. The blue trade wind, the gold trade wind caressing the bending canes.... City life, what had it done for any of them, after all? Edna a harlot (since she had left them there was no other word), and Charlie fast going to pieces, having joined the Promenade of a notorious Bar with its bright particular galaxy of boys.

" Sh'o, ebberyt'ing happier back dah," she mused, following the slow gait across the street of some bare-footed nuns; soon they would be returning, with many converts and pilgrims, to Sasabonsam, beyond the May Day Mountains, where remained a miraculous image of Our Lady of the Sorrows still intact. How if she joined them, too? A desire to express her grief, and thereby ease it, possessed her. In the old times there had been many ways: tribal dances, and wild austerities. . . .

She was still musing self-absorbed, when her mother, much later, came in from the street.

There had been a great Intercessional, it seemed, at the cathedral, with hired singers, from the Opera House and society women as thick as thieves, "*gnats*," she had meant to say (Tee-hee!) about a corpse. Arturo Arrivabene . . . a voice like a bull . . . and she had caught a glimpse of Edna driving on the Avenue Amanda, looking almost Spanish in a bandeau beneath a beautiful grey tilt hat.

But Miami's abstraction discouraged confidences.

"Why you so triste, chile? Dair no good, at all, in frettin'."

"Sh'o nuff."

"Dat death was on de cards my deah, an' dair is no mistakin' de fac ; an' as de shark is a rapid feeder it all ober sooner dan wid de crocodile, which is some consolation for dose dat remain to mourn."

"Sh'o, it bring not an attom to me! "

" 'Cos de process ob de crocodile bein' sloweh dan dat ob de shark — "

"Ah, say no more," Miami moaned, throwing herself in a storm of grief across the bed. And as all efforts to soothe, made matters only worse, Mrs. Mouth prudently left her.

" Prancing Nigger, she seem dat sollum-cholly an' depressed," Mrs. Mouth remarked at dinner, helping herself to some guava-jelly, that had partly dissolved through lack of ice.

" Since de disgrace ob Edna dat scarcely s'prisin'," Mr. Mouth made answer, easing a little napkin at his neck.

" She is her own woman me deah sah, an' *I* cannot prevent it! "

In the convivial ground-floor dining-room, " First-Greek-Empire " style, it was hard, at times, to endure such second-rate company, as that of a querulous husband.

Yes, marriage had its dull side, and its drawbacks, still, where would society be, (and where morality!) without the married women?

Mrs. Mouth fetched a sigh.

Just at her husband's back, above the ebony sideboard, hung a Biblical engraving after Rembrandt, *Woman Taken in Adultery,* the conception of which seemed to her exaggerated and overdone, knowing full well, from previous experience, that there need not, really, be much fuss. . . . Indeed, there need not be any: but to be *Taken* like that! A couple of idiots.

" Wen' I look at our chillens chairs, an' all ob dem empty, in my opinion, we both betteh deaded," Mr. Mouth brokenly said.

" I daresay dair are dose dat may t'ink so," Mrs. Mouth returned, refilling her glass, " but, Prancing Nigger, I am not like dat; no sah! "

" Where's Charlie? "

" I s'poge he choose to dine at de lil Cantonese restaurant on de quay," she murmured, setting down her glass with a slight grimace: how *ordinaire* this cheap red wine! Edna doubtless was sipping champagne! Respectability had its trials. . . .

" Dis jelly mo' like lemon squash," Mr. Mouth commented.

" 'Cos dat lil liard Ibum, he again forget de ice! Howebber, I hope soon to get rid ob him: for de insolence ob his bombax is more dan I can stand," Mrs. Mouth declared, lifting her voice on account of a piano-organ in the street just outside.

"I s'poge today Chuesd'y? It was a-Chuesd'y — God forgib dat po' frail chile."

"Prancing Nigger, I allow Edna some young yet for dat position; I allow dat to be de matteh ob de case but, me good sah! Bery likely she marry him later."

"Pah."

"An', why not?"

"Chooh, nebba!"

"Prancing Nigger, you seem to forget dat your elder daughter was a babe ob four, w'en I put on me nuptial arrange blastams to go to de Church."

"Sh'o, I wonder you care to talk ob it!"

"An', today, honey, as I sat in de Cathedral, lis'nin' to de Archbishop, I seemed to see Edna, an' she all in *dentelles* so *chic,* comin' up de aisle, followed by twelve maids, all ob good blood, holdin' flowehs an' wid hats kimpoged ob feddehs — worn raddeh to de side, and' I heah a stranger say: "Excuse me, sah, but who dis fine marriage?" an a voice make reply: "Why, dat Mr. Ruiz de milliona'r-'r-'r'," an' as he speak, one ob dese Italians from de Opera house, commence to sing, "De voice dat brieved o'er Eden," an' Edna she blow a kis at me an' laugh dat arch."

" Nebba! "

" Prancing Nigger, ' wait an' see '! " Mrs. Mouth waved prophetically her fan.

" No, nebba," he repeated, his head sunk low in chagrin.

" How you know, sah? " she queried, rising to throw a crust of loaf to the organ man outside.

The wind with the night had risen, and a cloud of blown dust was circling before the gate.

" See de rain drops, deah; here come at last de big rain."

" . . . ."

" Prancing Nigger! "

" Ah'm thinkin'."

XIV

IMPROVISING at the piano, Piltzen-hoffer, kiddy-grand, he was contented, happy. The creative fertility, bursting from a radiant heart, more than ordinary surprised him: " My most quickening affair, since — " he groped, smiling a little at several particular wraiths, more, or less, bizarre, that, in their time, had especially disturbed him. Yes; probably! " he murmured, enigmatically, striking an intricate, virile chord.

" Forgib me dearest! I was wid de manicu' of de fingehnails."

" Divine one."

She stood before him.

Hovering there between self-importance, and madcapery, she was exquisite quite.

" All temperament . . . ! " he murmured, capturing her deftly between his knees.

She was wearing a toilette of white *crêpe de chine,* and a large favour of bright purple Costa-Rica roses.

" Soon as de sun drop, dey set out, deah: so de manicu' say."

" What shall we do till then? "

" . . . or, de pistols! " she fluted, encircling an arm about his neck.

" Destructive kitten," he murmured, kissing, one by one her red, polished nails.

" Honey! Come on."

He frowned.

It seemed a treason almost to his late mistress, an exotic English girl, perpetually shivering, even in the sun, this revolver practice on the empty Quinine-bottles she had left behind. Poor Meraude. It was touching what faith she had had in a dose of quinine! Unquestionably she had been faithful to *that*. And, dull enough, too, it had made her. With her albums of photographs, nearly all of midshipmen, how insufferably had she bored him — : " This one, darling, tell me, isn't he — I, really — he makes me — and this one, darling! An Athenian viking, with hair like mimosa, and what ravishing hands! — oh my God! — I declare — he makes me — " Poor Meraude; she had been extravagant as well.

" Come on, an' break some bokkles! "

" There's not a cartridge left," he told her, setting her on his knee.

> "Ha-ha! Oh, hi-hi!
> Not a light;
> Not a bite!
> What a Saturday Night!"

she trilled, taking off a comedian from the Eden Garden.

Like all other negresses she possessed a natural bent for mimicry, and a voice of that lisping quality that would find complete expression in songs such as: Have you seen my sweet garden ob Flowehs? Sst! Come closter, Listen heah, Lead me to the Altar Dearest, and His Little Pink, proud, Spitting-lips are Mine.

" What is that you're wearing? "

" A souvenir ob today; I buy it fo' Luck," she rippled, displaying a black briar cross pinned to her breast.

" I hope it's blessed? "

" De nun dat sold it, didn't say: Sh'o, it's dreadful to t'ink ob po' Mimi, an' she soon a pilgrim all in blistehs an' rags," she commented, as a page boy with bejasmined ears appeared at the door.

" Me excuse. . . ."

" How dare you come in lil saucebox, widdout knockin'? "

" Excuse, missey, but . . . "

" What? "

Ibum hung his head.

" I only thoughted, it bein' Crucifix day, I would like to follow in de procession thu de town."

" Bery well: but be back in time fo' dinner."

" T'ank you, missey."

" An' mind fo' once you are! "

" Yes, missey," the niggerling acquiesced, bestowing a slow smile on Snob and Snowball who had accompanied him into the room. Easy of habit, as tropical animals are apt to be, it was apparent that the aristocratic pomeranian was paying sentimental court to the skittish mouser, who, since her περιπέτεια of black kittens looked ready for anything.

" Sh'o, but she hab a way wid her! " Ibum remarked impressed.

" Lil monster, take dem both, an' den get out ob my sight," his mistress directed him.

Fingering a battered volume, that bore the book-plate of Meraude, Vittorio appeared absorbed.

" Honey."

" Well? "

" Noddin'."

In the silence of the room, a restless bluebottle, attracted by the wicked leer of a chandalier, tied up incredibly in a bright green net, blended its hum with the awakening murmur of the streets.

" Po' Mimi. I hope she look up as she go by."

" Yes, by Jove."

" Doh after de rude t'ings she say to me — " she broke off, blinking a little at the sunlight through the thrilling shutters.

" If I remember, beloved, you were both equally candid," he remarked, wandering out upon the balcony.

It was on the palm grown Messalina, an avenue that comprised a solid portion of the Ruiz estate, that he had installed her, in a many-storied building, let out in offices and flats.

Little gold, blue, lazy and romantic Cuna, what chastened mood broods over thy life today?

" Have you your crucifix? Won't you buy a cross?" persuasive, feminine voices rose up from the pavement below. Active again with the waning sun, " workers," with replenished wares, were emerging forth from their respective dépots nursing small lugubrious baskets.

" Have you bought your cross?" The demand, when softly cooed, by some solicitous patrician, almost compelled an answer; and most of the social world of Cuna appeared to be vending crosses, or " Pilgrims' medals " in imitation " bronze," this afternoon upon the curb. At the corner of Valdez Street, across the way, Countess Kattie Taosay, (*née* Soderini), austere in black with Parma violets, was presiding over a dépot festooned with nothing but rosaries, that " professed " themselves, as they hung, to the suave trade-wind.

> "Not a light;
> Not a bite!
> What a——"

Edna softly hummed, shading her eyes with a big feather fan.

It was an evening of cloudless radiance; sweet and mellow as is frequent as the close of summer.

" Oh, ki, honey! It so cleah, I can see de lil iluns ob yalleh sand, far away b'yond de Point."

" Dearest! " he inattentively murmured, recognising on the Avenue the elegant cobweb wheels of his mother's Bolivian buggy.

Accompanied by Eurydice Edwards, she was driving her favourite mules.

" An' de shipwreck off de coral reef, oh, ki! "

" Let me find you the long-glass dear," he said, glad for an instant to step inside.

Leaning with one foot thrust nimbly out through the balcony-rails towards the street, she gazed absorbed.

Delegates of agricultural guilds bearing banners, making for the Cathedral square (the pilgrims starting-point), were advancing along the avenue amidst applause: fruit-growers, rubber-growers, sugar-growers, opium growers all doubtless wish-

ful of placating Nature that redoubtable
Goddess, by shewing a little honour to the
Church. " Oh Lord, *not* as Sodom," she
murmured, deciphering a text attached to
the windscreen of a luxurious automobile.

" Divine one, here they are."

" T'anks, honey, I see best widdout," she
replied, following the Bacchic progress of
two girls in soldier's forage-caps, who were
exciting the gaiety of the throng.

" Be careful, kid; don't lean too far...."

" Oh, ki, if dey don't exchange kisses! "

But the appearance of the Cunan Con-
stabulary, handsome youngsters, looking
the apotheosis themselves of earthly law-
lessness, in their feathered sun-hats and
bouncing kilts, created a diversion.

" De way dey stare up; I goin' to put on
a tiara! "

" Wait, do, till supper," he entreated,
manipulating the long-glass to suit his eye.

Driving or on foot, were the usual faces.

Seated on a doorstep, Miss Maxine Bush,
the famous actress, appeared to be rehears-
ing a smart society *rôle,* as she flapped the
air with a sheet of street-fowl paper, while

rattling a money-box, her tame monkey, "Jutland-ho," came as prompt for a coin as any demned Duchess.

"Ha-ha, Oh, hi-hi!" Edna's blasted catches: "Bless her," he exclaimed, re-levelling the glass. Perfect. Good lenses these; one could even read a physician's doorplate across the way: "Hours 2–4, Agony guaranteed" — obviously, a dentist, and the window-card too, above, " Miss — ? Miss — ?   Miss — ? — *Speciality:* Men past thirty."

Four years to wait. Patience.

Ooof! There went "Alice" and one of her boys. Bad days for the ballet! People afraid of the Opera house . . . that chandalier . . . and the pictures on the roof. . . . And wasn't that little Lady Bird? Running at all the trousers: "*have* you your crucifix! . . . ? ?"

"Honey. . . ."

She had set a crown of moonstones on her head, and had moonstone bracelets on her arms.

"My queen."

"I hope Mimi look up at me!"

" Vain one."

Over the glistering city the shadows were falling, staining the white-walled houses here and there as with some purple pigment.

" Accordin' to de lates' 'ticklers, de Procession follow de Paseo only as far as de fountain."

" Oh. . . ."

" Where it turn up thu Carmen street, into de Avenue Messalina."

Upon the metallic sheen of the evening sky, she sketched the itinerary, lightly with her fan.

And smiling down on her uplifted face, he asked himself whimsically how long he would love her. She had not the brains poor child of course to keep a man forever. Heigho. Life indeed was often hard. . . .

" Honey, here dey come! "

A growing murmur of distant voices, jointly singing, filled liturgically, the air, together as the warning salute, fired at sundown, from the fort heights, above the town, reverberated sadly.

" Oh, la, la," she laughed, following the

wheeling flight of some birds that rose
startled from the palms.

" The Angelus. . . ."

" Hark, honey: What is dat dey singin? "

A thousand ages in Thy sight
Are like an evening gone,
Short as the watch that ends the night
Before the rising sun.

Led by an old negress leaning on her
hickory staff, the procession came.

Banners, banners, banners.

" I hope Mimi wave! "

Floating banners against the dusk. . . .

" Oh, honey! See dat lil pilgrim-boy? "

Time like an ever-rolling stream,
Bears all its sons away;
They fly forgotten, as a dream
Dies at the opening day.

" Mimi, Mimi! " She had flung the roses
from her dress: " Look up, my deah, look
up."

But her cry escaped unheard.

They fly forgotten, as a dream
Dies——

The echoing voices of those behind lingered a little.

" Edna."

She was crying.

" It noddin'; noddin', at all! But it plain she refuse to forgib me! "

" Never,"

" Perspirin', an' her skirt draggin', sh'o, she looked a fright."

He smiled: For indeed already the world was perceptibly moulding her. . . .

" Enuff to scare ebbery crow off de Savannah! "

" And wouldn't the Farmers bless her."

" Oh, honey! " Her glance embraced the long, lamp-lit avenue with suppressed delight.

" Well."

" Dair's a new dancer at de Apollo, to-night. Suppose we go? "

A Chronology of Ronald Firbank

1886: Arthur Annesley Ronald Firbank, son of Thomas and Harriette Firbank, is born at 40 Clarges Street, London, on 17 January some six months before his grandfather's death. Joseph Firbank, the grandfather, had begun his professional career as a coal miner in the Durham pits at the age of seven, had become a railway labourer at twenty-one, and had risen with remarkable energy and acumen to become one of England's wealthiest railway contractors. His son Thomas was a socially ambitious man, conventional and "very keen on all outdoor sports." His honours included positions as Justice of the Peace, Deputy Lieutenant, Member of Parliament, and High Sheriff of Monmouthshire; eventually he was knighted. After his marriage to the daughter of an Irish clergyman, he became a connoisseur of the arts and a collector of porcelains. Mrs. Firbank, later Lady Firbank, was a doting mother who both spoiled and dominated her children, especially Ronald. Her first child had been a son, Joseph Sydney; after Ronald she bore another son, Hubert Somerset, and a daughter, Heather.

1887-99: Ronald's boyhood until 1896 is part of a closely knit family life. The Firbank children exchange invitations to tea. When they are old enough, they swim, play golf, and ride. They make extensive visits with their parents and servants to fashionable resorts in England, and they travel abroad. Each boy collects something; in Ronald's case it is books and autographs. In 1896 Ronald—he is called "Artie" at this time—is a special student at the Mortimer Vicarage School, Eton, Bucks. In this year he writes a novel, *Lila*, and two years later, *"Lady Appledore's Mesalliance"* (*An Artificial Pastoral*) and probably the poem *The Fairies Wood*.

1900-03: Ronald's schooling is varied: In December 1900 he enters a robust public school, Uppingham, and remains until April 1901. Then, in May, he commences study under a private tutor at Park Holm, Buxton, Derbyshire and continues until 2 June. In September he moves to Howley Grange, Sainte-Tulle, Basses-Alpes, where he receives instruction until Christmas. Meanwhile his parents, inspired perhaps by the knighthood conferred on the elder Firbank at King Edward's coronation in 1902, decree that Ronald's talents are best suited to the diplomatic service, and he goes in October 1903 to Le Mortier de St. Symphorien, Indre et Loire to perfect his French. As always, however, he is writing. He completes two plays in 1900, *A Disciple from the Country* (*A Comedy in I Act*) and *The Mauve Tower* (*A Dream Play in VII Scenes*). And he reads, especially the French writers who will influence his whole literary career.

1904: Ronald continues at St. Symphorien until August and then, still preparing for the diplomatic examinations, removes to Paris (17, rue Tronchet) until the end of the year. In Paris he writes the incomplete *Far Away*, vaguely suggestive of his later work, and he publishes for the first time: "La Princesse aux Soleils," written in English and translated by the author, appears in the November issue of "*Les Essais.*" This stay in France encourages his attachment to the "cult of the purple orchid." Ronald's older brother, "Joey," dies in November in his twenty-first year, and now Lady Firbank binds Ronald more closely to her.

1905: Three Firbank publications appear. The February issue of "*Les Essais*" carries *Harmonie*. His first book, containing *Odette* and *A Study in Temperament*, is brought out in June by Elkin Mathews; Firbank pays for the cost of producing this as he is to do with almost all his books. In December "Souvenir d'automne" appears in the Supplement to *The King and His Navy and Army*. Only *A Study in Temperament* indicates how Firbank's writing will develop. He is intensely interested in *fin de siècle* literature of France and England. He is now collecting rare editions of Oscar Wilde and others, and he reads Verlaine and Ernest Dowson for the first time. Ronald continues his education with a stay in Madrid which lasts from 22 February until 6 July. There he occupies quarters in a pension at 92 Calle Mayor run by a Miss Briggs. He entertains lavishly in rooms heavy with silks, incense, and candle fumes. A Spanish friend of the period described him: "*Alto, rubio, delgado y un poco presumtuoso, aunque con chic, un tanto afectadillo.*" On leaving Spain he returns to England and in October enters Scoones', a "cramming house" in London. During his stay there he indulges his taste for opera and the theatre. But this activity ends some time before Christmas, and in late December after a short holiday in Paris, Firbank is at The Parsonage, Bielside, Aberdeenshire. He is now being tutored for Cambridge.

1906: Firbank remains at Bielside until 20 June. He then goes to The Vicarage, St. Peter's-in-Thanet until 10 August. And on 12 October he goes up to Trinity Hall, Cambridge. He promptly submits " 'The Wavering Disciple.' A Fantasia." to *The Granta,* an undergraduate publication, and it appears in two parts (24 November and 5 December). He is developing his own subject and method in the general vein of *A Study in Temperament.*

1907-09: In spite of his father's serious financial reverses in 1907, Firbank leads a leisurely and luxurious life at Cambridge, with frequent excursions to the London theatre. His second *Granta* publication, "A Study in Opal," comes out in the 2 November issue. In 1908 Monsignor Hugh Benson receives him into the Roman Church. Benson makes him row and thus somewhat a part of a rowing college which went "Head of the River" in these years. But Firbank is more concerned with the image he imposes on his friends, as a man of the world intimate with the arts and their creators. He sits for no examinations, and he leaves the university in June 1909 after completing only five of the required nine terms. He talks of entering the Vatican Service.

1910-12: Unable to secure an appointment at the Vatican, Firbank feels, as Lord Berners later reported, that the Church has rejected him. This attitude will colour his fiction. Sir Thomas Firbank dies in 1910. His father had recouped enough of his fortune after 1907 for Lady Firbank and Ronald to take up residence in Curzon Street in near luxury. He begins to advise his mother in financial matters. And as usual he is writing. He will later name eight plays or short stories, besides those published, which he wrote between 1900 and 1911. This year he visits Egypt for the first time. He travels also to Constantinople, Vienna, Rome, Florence, and Paris.

1913-14: Ronald enters "Smart Bohemia": he becomes a frequent patron of Stulik's Eiffel Tower in Percy Street and of the Café Royal. He makes the acquaintance of Augustus John, Thomas Earp, Evan Morgan, and others. Determined to discipline himself, he begins *Vainglory* in 1913. It is nearly finished by mid-summer, 1914; so he goes to the Continent for a holiday. He pauses in Paris long enough to consult an astrologer about the future of his book. He then goes to Italy and is there when war is declared. Firbank finally returns to England and after visits to York and Edinburgh, he settles in Oxford, in rooms in the High opposite Longwall. He offers *Vainglory* for publication late in December. His only surviving brother, "Bertie," dies in this year.

1915: Grant Richards publishes *Vainglory*, at the author's expense, with a frontispiece by Felicien Rops. On the title page, Firbank styles himself "Ronald" for the first time, but "A.A.R. Firbank" appears on the book's dust jacket. He begins *Inclinations*.

1916: *Inclinations* comes out in June with a frontispiece, tail-piece, and dust jacket designed by William Rutherston. A revised version of *Odette* with four illustrations by Albert Buhrer is published in December. Firbank continues at Oxford with visits to London and Torquay. He is writing *Caprice*.

1917: *Caprice* is published with a frontispiece drawing by Augustus John. In the summer Firbank starts work on *Valmouth*. He continues to live in Oxford. He serves one day in the army and then receives a certificate of discharge dated Oxford, 11 June.

1918: Firbank continues at Oxford with visits to London. He is still at work on *Valmouth*.

1919: Early in the year Ronald is honoured with a dinner party at the Golden Cross Inn, Oxford. Osbert Sitwell, his brother Sacheverell and Siegfried Sassoon have invited the guests to hear Firbank read from *Valmouth*. As a result, Osbert arranges for the publication of a chapter from the book in *Art and Letters*. Ronald returns to London, takes rooms in Jermyn Street, and is seen once more at the Eiffel Tower, the Café Royal, first nights, and exhibition galleries. He drinks excessively. His eccentricities become more pronounced. And his dress is conspicuous; his suits are dark, his hat the "Trilby," but according to Evan Morgan his shirts are in colours rarely seen off the stage and his ties "very bohemian." His writing goes on without interruption. *Valmouth*, with a frontispiece by Augustus John, is issued in November.

1920: The appearance of *Valmouth* brings new friends such as Nancy Cunard, Nina Hamnett, Aldous Huxley, Wyndham Lewis, and others. Firbank travels by way of Paris and Marseilles to North Africa—Constantine, Algiers, Kairouan, Tunis—where he spends the winter. In November Grant Richards publishes *The Princess Zoubaroff*, a play never acted during Firbank's lifetime. Firbank is at work on *Santal* and already planning *The Flower Beneath the Foot*.

1921: He remains in Tunis until March, when he goes to Italy. In June, having returned to London, Firbank arranges for the publication of *Santal*. It appears in September. Meanwhile he is settled at Versailles, where he begins to write *The Flower Beneath the Foot*. He continues his work on the book when he moves to Switzerland for the winter.

1922: Firbank goes from Montreux to Florence at the end of February. There, in May, he completes *The Flower Beneath the Foot*. In late summer he sets off for Cuba and Jamaica in search of materials for another book. He finds them in Cuba. He returns to London and goes on to Bordighera to start work on *Sorrow in Sunlight*. His health is declining. His diet and addiction to alcohol do not help, and the smallest exertion or least excitement brings on asthmatic attacks.

1923: Firbank remains at Bordighera until mid-summer with occasional visits elsewhere such as the one to Monte Carlo, where he goes to dine with Lily Langtry as the guest of his publisher Grant Richards. He is still at Bordighera when *The Flower Beneath the Foot*, with a decoration by C. R. W. Nevinson and portraits by Augustus John and Wyndham Lewis, is published. Ronald is in touch with admirers in New York. Carl Van Vechten had written about Firbank in *The Double Dealer* and now arranges publication in *The Reviewer* of one chapter from Firbank's new novel. Van Vechten and Stuart Rose make it possible for Brentano's, New York, to publish *Sorrow in Sunlight*. Toward the end of summer Firbank goes to Spain and in Seville conceives his next novel which will be called *Concerning the Eccentricities of Cardinal Pirelli*. He starts it in December after he is settled in Rome.

1924: Brentano's publishes *Sorrow in Sunlight*, renamed *Prancing Nigger* by Carl Van Vechten. Ronald hardly notices its production in his intense grief at the death of his mother. After attending her funeral, very ill, he returns to Rome and continues work on *Cardinal Pirelli*. An American edition of *The Flower Beneath the Foot* with the author's preface comes out in New York, a part of an American edition of Firbank's works projected but never completed by Brentano's. The London branch publishes *Sorrow in Sunlight* under its original name.

1925: Still in Rome, Firbank completes *Cardinal Pirelli* in February. He immediately writes a preface for *Caprice* and rewrites the "dinner party" chapter of *Inclinations* with a view to American editions. Neither is published. He revises *Vainglory* for autumn publication in America. In spring Firbank is in London, his health seriously impaired. He goes to Arcachon and then to Cairo. There at the end of the year he starts a novel about New York named *The New Rythum*.

1926: Before leaving Cairo in February Firbank complains of having caught a cold. In Rome his health does not improve and there, at the Hotel Quirinale, he dies on 21 May. He is buried in the Protestant Cemetery; his sister will later have his body disinterred and placed in the Catholic Cemetery at San Lorenzo. After Firbank's death Grant Richards publishes *Concerning the Eccentricities of Cardinal Pirelli*. His most complex book, it emphasises his repeated comment on the anarchy man's self-involvement has made of traditions, institutions, the whole order of inherited values.

The man behind the myth which he did so much to create is plainly visible in the numerous letters and other documents preserved by his mother and sister. Ronald Firbank emerges as a careful, uncompromising artist whose existence was shaped by his determination to write.

MIRIAM J. BENKOVITZ